PLAYING MUM

Freya Hardy's sister Astrid has been called for jury service, so she offers to take care of her two nieces and nephew while putting her travelling plans on hold. But Freya soon discovers that being a stand-in mum is much harder than being an auntie . . . Jamie Barnes, deputy head at her nephew's school, is unimpressed with Freya's efforts, and the two of them clash — but when Jamie steps in to help during a crisis, their relationship changes. And when Astrid returns, Freya has a decision to make about her future . . .

SARAH PURDUE

PLAYING MUM

Complete and Unabridged

LINFORD
Leicester

First published in Great Britain in 2017

First Linford Edition
published 2017

A catalogue record for this book is available
from the British Library.

ISBN 978–1–4448–3510–6

Published by
F. A. Thorpe (Publishing)
Anstey, Leicestershire

Set by Words & Graphics Ltd.
Anstey, Leicestershire
Printed and bound in Great Britain by
T. J. International Ltd., Padstow, Cornwall

This book is printed on acid-free paper

1

The screaming seemed to be reaching its crescendo. Freya was now reasonably sure that they couldn't continue for much longer. Nothing as small as the child in front of her could possibly sustain that level of noise for any length of time, surely?

She rubbed a hand across her temple to try and ease some of the strain from her forehead, which she knew from reading in magazines was a sure and certain way to get wrinkles. Her phone rang in her pocket; not that she could hear it over the noise, but she could feel the vibrations. She pulled it out, saw who the caller was, and took her opportunity to step further away from the source of the noise, which was now rolling around on the floor, angry limbs flailing.

'Hi, sis,' Freya said, shoving the index

finger of her free hand in her ear so that she could hear better. 'How's jury service in the big smoke?'

There was a pause, and Freya was sure the background noise had travelled down the phone line the two-hundred-odd miles to where Astrid was, in London.

'Is that screaming I can hear?'

Freya winced. Lying to her sister was not an option. Astrid had practically raised her and had a mother's instinct for the truth. 'Yep. I'm at the supermarket and some poor child is having a meltdown.' Freya crossed the fingers that weren't in her left ear in a childlike attempt to ward off the tiny white lie she had just uttered.

There was another pause, which Freya knew was an ominous omen. Then: 'Would that happen to be *my* child screaming?'

Freya could practically hear one of Astrid's eyebrows rising. She tried one last stab at deflection. 'What makes you say that?'

'I'd recognise those dulcet tones anywhere. Put her on the phone.' And there it was — the no-nonsense tone that Freya had not managed to master in her twenty-five years on the planet.

'I'm not sure Daisy's really in a condition to talk to you,' Freya said, wincing as the tantrum-related screams seemed to increase in pitch.

'Tell her it's me,' Astrid said in a monotone.

'Okay.' Freya tried a cheery 'this really isn't bothering me at all' voice. With a sigh she sidled back to Daisy, who was beginning to draw a large disapproving crowd whose murmured criticisms were loud enough for Freya to make out. 'Uh, Daisy honey?'

Daisy did not so much as pause for breath; she just looked Freya straight in the eye before throwing her head back and yelling some more.

'It's your mummy on the phone.' Tentatively Freya held out the phone in the toddler's general direction. Freya blinked, wondering if her fairy godmother had stealthily approached and waved her magic wand. Not only had Daisy stopped yelling, but she had pulled herself up on her chubby little legs, brushed the hair from her tear-stained face, and grabbed the phone from her aunt's outstretched hand.

'Hello, Mummy!' she squealed, moving from total meltdown to 'butter would melt in less than two seconds'. All Freya could do was stare and be grateful that the disapproving crowd was moving away, albeit still muttering about poor parenting skills. As she watched her youngest niece talk on the phone, she knew she had no parenting skills, of course she didn't. She was, however, an excellent auntie, or at least she had thought she was until five minutes ago when a refusal to buy sweets had caused such an epic meltdown.

'Mummy wants to talk to you,' Daisy said, smiling sweetly and handing Freya back her phone.

'Whatever magic words you used, I want to learn them,' Freya said gratefully into the phone.

'You just have to be firm with her, Freya. That's all. Remember, for the next two weeks you're the stand-in mummy, not the auntie. I know usually you get to do all the fun stuff, but now it's time to get serious.'

Freya knew her sister was trying not to laugh. 'You're loving this, aren't you?' she hissed into the phone, hoping that Daisy couldn't hear her.

'No, of course not,' Astrid said before dissolving into giggles.

Freya gave her a moment to have her laugh. 'You were right, it's not as easy as it looks.' She turned her attention back to Daisy just as she knocked over a cardboard display unit, causing several hundred oranges to cascade across the floor. Freya's eyes widened as she saw a very upset store manager heading her way.

'Got to go, sis. Talk to you later.' She hung up on her sister, who was clearly too busy laughing to offer any further parenting wisdom, and turned to the store manager. 'I am so sorry. I literally took my eyes off her for a second.'

The older woman crossed her arms across her chest, and Freya was fairly sure she was in for a lengthy telling-off.

'I'll pick them all up,' she said hurriedly, lifting up the cardboard stand, which now listed heavily to the right. 'And of course pay for any damages.'

★ ★ ★

Freya and Daisy left the store with Freya's wallet twenty pounds lighter and the pushchair weighed down with two shopping bags full of bruised fruit.

'Well that went well,' she said to Daisy, who she had sat back in her pushchair and ensured she was strapped in so there could be no more bolts for freedom, which enviably seemed to lead to a one-toddler crime spree. Her phone beeped again, and with a groan she glanced at her watch. They were going to be late again. 'Hold tight, Daisy. We're going to have to make a run for it.'

In the last week, Freya had become an expert at the pushchair gauntlet on the hill that led up to the small village primary school. She had had plenty of practice in fighting against the tide of pushchairs, small uniformed children and mothers heading in the opposite direction. However hard she tried, she could not get both children ready to go in time for the leisurely walk that every other mother in the village seemed to manage without working up a sweat.

She ignored the raised eyebrows and dark looks, keeping her head down and her feet moving. When she reached the main gates to the school, she saw the small figure of her nephew Benji sitting on a low wall, kicking his feet and looking dejected.

'Hi, Benji!' She took one hand off the pushchair to wave at him, and it wobbled and nearly clipped the school gates. 'Sorry we're late, buddy. Daisy had a full-on tantrum in the shop.'

'Again?' her nephew said, lifting his head, and Freya could see fat tears rolling down his cheeks. Freya wasn't sure if he was commenting on her lateness or her inability to deal with Daisy's tantrums.

She carefully put the brakes on the pushchair and went to sit beside him. He sniffed, wiped his nose on the sleeve of his sweatshirt, and then looked up at her. 'Mr Barnes wants to see you,' he said with another sniff.

'Does he?' Freya said, trying to keep her voice light. She hated to see Benji so upset, and hated it more knowing that she was the cause. 'Well, I'll call him tomorrow and make an appointment. I'll sort all this out, Benji, I promise.'

'Perhaps you could make some time in your busy schedule now?'

Freya flinched, and for a second she was wishing her fairy godmother could make him disappear just like Cinderella had at the stroke of midnight. But when she looked up he was still standing there, handsome as ever, looking down at her. When he saw he had her attention, he held his arm out in the direction of the school building that housed his office.

'Sure,' Freya said brightly; but with every step she knew she was in for another telling-off. There was nothing quite like being summoned to the head teacher's office.

2

Freya followed Mr Barnes meekly into the entrance hall, passing display boards of artwork and poetry, pushing Daisy and trying to get Benji to smile. Her five-year-old nephew looked so miserable that there and then Freya made a silent promise to herself and him that whatever happened, whatever catastrophe, tomorrow they would be on time.

When they reached Mr Barnes's office, he pressed a button on his desk, and an older lady stepped out of a small side office. 'Mrs Jones, could you keep an eye on Benji and Daisy for a minute while I have a word with Miss . . . ' He left Freya's title hanging.

'Hardy. Freya Hardy,' Freya said, unable to ignore the question. She turned and tried a smile on Mrs Jones, and for the first time that day the smile was returned.

'Come on, Benji — you can help me with the photocopying. You're such a good helper, and I have so much to do. It's wonderful that you're here.'

Benji sniffed and nodded, his little face still serious but also purposeful. Freya did her best to transmit how grateful she was to Mrs Jones, who was clearly one of those people who just seemed to naturally know the exact right thing to say in any given moment. Mrs Jones winked at her and Freya smiled, relieved to feel like perhaps she had one ally in this alien place.

Freya was suddenly aware that in the seconds she had spent conveying her unspoken message to Mrs Jones, she was keeping Mr Barnes waiting. For his part, he was standing there holding the door open for her, and she couldn't read his expression, but she imagined it was yet another black mark against her name.

'Miss Hardy, please pull up a chair.'

Freya looked around her. In front of the large wooden desk, which was covered in paper, picture frames and what looked like the remainders of Mr Barnes's lunch, there was a row of small chairs. Not just small chairs, but the kind you find in nursery school. Freya looked up from the chairs, but Mr Barnes had his back to her; and, not knowing what else to do, she walked round to one of the tiny chairs and sat down. At nearly five foot seven, sitting on one of these chairs meant that her knees were literally round her ears. She began to wonder if this was one of those tricks that you learned at headmaster school — 'Ways to make parents feel small, literally and figuratively'.

Mr Barnes turned and sat down in his own black executive office chair. Or at least Freya assumed that was what he had done, since from her position she couldn't actually see over the desk. But as quickly as he had sat down, he stood up again, and Freya could hear the chair spring back to its original height.

'Miss Hardy . . . ' He looked both

aghast and confused. ' . . . what are you doing?'

From her angle of view, Mr Barnes seemed like a giant, even though he was probably six feet tall; and Freya wondered if that was how Benji felt when he stood in front of the head teacher. It was not a comfortable place to be. 'You asked me to sit down,' she said, wondering if this was all part of his plan to make her feel even more uncomfortable.

Mr Barnes stared at her as if she was a duck that had wandered in off the street and had no idea how it had found itself in the head teacher's office. 'I meant one of those seats,' he said, indicating with his arm to two adult-sized chairs. 'We had circle time recently,' he said faintly, and Freya knew that he was even more concerned about her being in charge of her nieces and nephew than ever before.

'Of course,' she mumbled, attempting to elegantly stand up from the tiny chair as if it was the most natural mistake in the world. She felt her knees creak with the effort and the right one let out a loud pop, which she thought made her sound as if she was at least eighty years old. She turned away from the desk on the pretext of collecting one of the normal-sized chairs and tried to compose herself. Why was life so embarrassing? she inwardly wailed. She was just trying to be a good sister and help Astrid out. She was just trying to be a good auntie ... Her mind switched briefly back to the conversation with Astrid. Her sister was right — for the next two weeks she was stand-in mum, and she needed to act like it.

Setting her face in what she hoped was a neutral expression, she placed the chair in front of the desk and sat down, crossing her legs at the ankle and folding her hands in her lap. She was pretty sure she had been told that this was the way to sit in an interview, and under the circumstances it seemed appropriate. Mr Barnes waited for her to be settled, and she was slightly nonplussed by the way he continued to stare at her as if he wasn't quite sure what to make of her.

'Mr Barnes,' Freya said, deciding the quickest and most painless way to get out of the office and away from yet another embarrassing moment was to take charge, 'my apologies for Benji's lateness this week. We're all having a little trouble adjusting to my sister being away, but I can assure you that it won't happen again.'

'That's what you said on Tuesday, Miss Hardy, and Benji has continued to be late.'

Freya opened her mouth to speak, but Mr Barnes held up a hand to stop her. It was such a teacher-move that Freya was fairly sure it would work on most under-eights. It riled her a little; but with her goal in mind of presenting herself as a fully grown adult who was more than capable of looking after three children, she decided to keep her mouth closed.

'What concerns me more is the fact that Benji has been the last child to leave the school all week. Yesterday I considered driving him to his home address myself; but since I couldn't contact you on the phone, I had no way of knowing if you'd be there to receive him.' He sat back in his chair and continued to stare at her. Again Freya was fairly sure this worked with the children.

'Just a few teething issues with the children's schedules. I have it sorted now.'

Mr Barnes raised an eyebrow — a very handsome eyebrow, now Freya came to think about it. That was before an image of Astrid swam before her eyes and told her to focus.

'So you've arranged for someone to be at home when Lily arrives on the school bus?'

Freya's eyes widened in panic. Despite her best attempts at being a responsible adult, she had managed to do it again. She had forgotten one of them. She could see Lily standing on the doorstep and no doubt rolling her eyes in that pre-teen way all eleven-year-olds seemed to possess, posting about her incompetent aunt on social media.

'I really have to go,' Freya said, standing up and heading for the door before Mr Barnes could admonish her further. 'Benji will be on time tomorrow. In fact, we'll be early. That's a promise.' She had her hand on the door handle and was certain she had made her escape.

'Please do see that Benji *is* here on time, Miss Hardy, or I'll have to contact Mrs Morse and ask if she can make more suitable arrangements.'

Freya's hand froze on the door handle as she fought down her anger. Was he seriously going to drop her in it with her sister? That was almost as bad as threatening to call a person's mother. The anger faded quickly and was replaced with an icy calmness. Who did this man think he was? She knew from the gossip at the gates that Mr Barnes was the village's most eligible bachelor and that he didn't have any children. Who was he to lecture her?

'I can assure you that won't be necessary,' she said, managing a haughty tone that her friends would be proud of.

3

With Benji running alongside, holding on to the pushchair, they made their way at a jog back down the hill and towards home. Freya's phone beeped several times, and she was fairly sure it would be Lily asking where she was. She thought about pausing to reply, but the truth was she couldn't bear to send another text saying she would be late, and it would only take ten minutes or so at a run to reach the large family house where her sister had set up home.

'Did you have fun with Mrs Jones?' Freya asked, hoping to strike up a conversation with Benji.

He stared at her, mouth open, panting with the effort of trying to keep up with her much longer legs. Freya forced herself to slow just a little, torn between not wanting to leave Lily on the doorstep for too long and not wanting Benji to collapse with fatigue.

'Sorry, buddy. I forget my legs are a bit longer than yours.' She grinned in the hope of getting some sort of positive response. Nothing. 'I was thinking we could watch one of those science programmes you like tonight. Just you and me? I'm sure Lily will have homework, and Daisy could do with an early night.'

Usually that would do the trick, or at least it always had before; but to Freya's horror Benji's face screwed up and she recognised the signs. He was trying not to cry, again. She felt ice in the pit of her stomach. She really was no good at this parenting thing.

She stopped now, knowing that she couldn't keep jogging on and ignoring him. Keeping one hand on the pushchair to prevent it rolling away from her as it had several times before, she reached out for him and pulled him into a tight hug. 'I'm so sorry, Benji. I promise I'll do better.' She could feel his small body shake with the effort of trying to stop his tears.

'You said I could talk to Mummy tonight.' The words came out shaky and were punctuated by sobs.

Freya realised her mistake. On Tuesday Astrid had been tied up until past Benji's bedtime, and she had used the 'science programme distraction technique' then. She leaned back, holding her nephew away from her so that she could see his face. 'You can still do that, sweetheart. Mummy's going to ring after we've had tea. I promise.'

'But you said . . . ' Benji's voice was still shaky, but there was a light in his eyes that hadn't been there before.

'I thought we could do that after,' Freya said, trying out a smile which thankfully was returned. She leaned in to pretend to whisper in his ear. 'I also thought we could make some of my amazing ice-cream sundaes, but you have to promise not to tell Mummy.'

Benji finally gave her a broad smile. 'With sprinkles?' he whispered as if he was sharing something top secret.

Freya nodded and pressed a finger to her lips. He giggled, and Freya didn't think she had ever been so happy to make her nephew laugh.

'We better go — Lily will be waiting,' Benji said, his grin slipping a little.

'Don't worry, I can handle Lily,' Freya said in what she hoped was an airy confident tone, knowing that she was trying to convince herself as much as Benji.

When they walked up the path, across the immaculate front gardens which were thanks to a local gardener, Freya could see that there was a torn-out piece of notebook stuck to the front door. When Freya and the younger children had been late home on Monday, Lily had made a big thing of packing a notebook and sticky tape in her bag so that she could leave Freya a note to say where she was, since she claimed Freya never answered her phone, like most 'old' people.

Over the last four days, Freya had

wondered what had happened to her sweet, fun-loving niece. She had even asked Astrid about it, who just laughed and said something about the teenage years starting early, and then went on to regale Freya with stories about what she had been like as a teenager. Freya, who had heard this all before, stopped listening and made up an excuse to get off the phone.

She pulled the note off the door and read it out loud. 'Gone to Steph's. Her mum says she is happy for me to stay with them for two weeks if you can't cope with all three of us. Have packed a bag. See you when Mum gets back. Lily (Your Niece).' Freya could feel her eyebrow raise at the tone and decided the first thing she would do once she got the other two settled was to ring Lily and tell her to get herself back home *tout de suite*.

'Right — inside, you two. Go and play while I get the tea ready.' She released Daisy from the pushchair, and both children headed for the playroom.

Freya manhandled the pushchair in through the front door, having never mastered the art of folding it down, and parked it in front of the downstairs toilet. She headed to the kitchen and switched on the oven before pulling out her phone and calling Lily. The phone was picked up after five rings, and Freya started her unrehearsed speech, only to be interrupted by a message.

'Hi, this is Lily. I'm busy right now, but you know what to do.' The beep made Freya jump.

'Lily, this is your aunt.' *Two can play at this game*, Freya thought. 'You need to come home right now.' She frowned to herself that this was going to work, since she was actually speaking to Lily. 'You need to come home as soon as you get this message. Tea will be at five thirty. Don't be late.' She winced slightly, knowing that the last comment was highly hypocritical. 'Don't make me call your mother.' She hung up before she could be given the option of re-recording her message.

Feeling guilty but not knowing what else to do, she pulled out the shepherd's pie from the fridge and put it in the oven. Astrid, as if knowing that there was no way that Freya could look after the children *and* prepare a nutritious dinner, had filled the freezer with meals before she'd headed to London for jury service.

Five thirty came and went. Daisy, Benji and Freya ate their tea, but there was no sign of Lily. Freya knew that it might be because Lily had not listened to her message; but it was more likely that her niece, who was never more than two seconds away from her phone, had checked her messages and decided to ignore it.

The phone rang, and Benji was answering it before the second ring. 'Mummy!' he said, and Freya smiled and left him to it. Astrid would sort things out — she always managed it; and even if she was two hundred miles away, she could work her magic. Freya settled on the sofa with Daisy, reading her favourite book to her.

'Mummy's coming home next week-end!' Benji yelled from the kitchen.

Freya let out a sigh of relief. 'You hear that, Daisy? Mummy will be home in eight sleeps.' Daisy bounced on her lap, but then pointed a chubby finger at the words in the book, which Freya took as a sign that she should keep reading.

'Mummy wants to talk to you,' Benji said, handing Freya the phone. She looked from it to Daisy.

'I can finish the story,' Benji said; he had a reading age far beyond his years. Freya watched as the two happily settled down together, and lifted the phone to her ear.

'So you've had quite a day,' Astrid said, and Freya knew that Benji had told her everything.

'Yep. It's been a while since I've been summoned to the head teacher's office for a telling-off,' Freya said with a grin. Now she was no longer in the office, it did seem quite funny.

'You really do need to get Benji there on time, Frey. You know how he gets.' Astrid's words were soft, and Freya knew that they contained no criticism, but somehow that was worse.

'I know. We'll be there on time tomorrow, I promise.' She mentally set her alarm clock for five a.m. Surely that would be enough time?

'And I hear Lily's decamped to Steph's.'

Freya could tell that she was smiling. 'Yep,' she said ruefully, 'another parenting fail on my part. We were a bit late getting back and she left me a note.'

'Did she, now?' Astrid said, and Freya knew that Lily was in trouble.

'She suggested that she could stay at Steph's until you got home. Apparently Steph's mum's okay with it.'

'That may be true, but *I'm* not, and I won't have my eleven-year-old making decisions without asking me — or you, for that matter. Lily will be home within the hour.'

'If you're thinking of phoning her, I

don't think that will work. She didn't answer my call.'

'Parenting 101, Freya: bypass the child. I'll ring Jan, Steph's mum, and ask her to drop Lily back to you so you don't have to take Daisy and Benji out again. Also, I'll be telling Lily she's grounded this weekend. No going out, no phones and no internet.'

'Isn't that a bit harsh? The kids are all missing you, you know.'

'I know, but that's not an excuse for Lily's behaviour. You've got to be strict on this one, Freya, or else when Lily actually gets to her teenage years there'll be hell to pay.'

4

When the doorbell rang, Freya was certain she didn't have the energy for any more battles. She had managed to wrestle Daisy into bed on her fifth attempt, and although she wasn't asleep — she was talking to her teddy bear — Freya had decided that was good enough for her. The doorbell meant that Lily was back, and so was her teenage attitude. Benji pressed pause on the remote and looked so worried that Freya had to smile just to reassure him.

'You carry on watching,' she said. 'You can catch me up in a minute.' Benji looked doubtful. 'I'm serious. I want to know how ants know where home is as much as you do.' He shrugged and pressed play while Freya carefully closed the door behind her. Whatever happened next, it was likely to be loud, and she preferred Benji not to be subjected to another display of her ineptitude.

She allowed herself a moment to compose herself and pulled open the door. Lily stood there with an expression that would make a Navy Seal quake in his boots. She was holding a suitcase. Freya nearly laughed out loud. Her niece clearly hadn't been joking when she said she had packed her things for two weeks.

'Lily,' she said brightly, 'welcome home. Why don't you go and put your stuff back upstairs.'

Behind Lily was a smartly dressed woman who looked like she must have an important job, as a solicitor or something. Once Lily had stomped off of the doorstep and into the house, the woman held out her hand and Freya shook it.

'You must be Freya. I'm Jan, Stephanie's mum. I'm really sorry about all this.' And to Freya she looked like she meant it, which caught her off guard. Could there be another person in this village who didn't have parenting sorted?

'Thanks, but I'm pretty sure this is all due to the girls,' Freya said with a smile. 'And me,' she added guiltily. 'I'm having trouble getting to grips with the scheduling, but I'm working on it.'

Jan laughed. 'I've been working on it for sixteen years and I don't think I've ever successfully managed the balance. Steph told me that you'd happily agreed to the arrangement, and between cooking dinner and collecting the boys from football I hadn't had the chance to check, so like a fool said it was all fine. Which it would be, of course, but I don't want to step on any toes.'

'Believe me, you're not, but Astrid is pretty keen to make sure that Lily knows she isn't the boss round here.'

'I know the feeling. I can't believe that at eleven years old they think they know everything. I'm sure I didn't have this trouble with the boys. Anyway, better get back to them to make sure they haven't re-mortgaged the house to buy more video games or something. If you need any help with anything, just give me a call.'

'Thanks — and thanks for looking after Lily. I'm going to be more organised from now on.'

Jan laughed once more and shouted, 'Good luck!' as she got into her car.

Freya watched her drive away, trying to delay the inevitable conversation she was going to have to have with Lily. With a sigh she closed the front door and walked up the stairs, feeling like she was going to meet her doom. A quick peek into Daisy's room showed that she had finally fallen asleep, sprawled across her toddler bed with the covers kicked off. Quietly Freya crept in, pulled up the covers and kissed Daisy's forehead, marvelling at how cute small children could be when they were asleep.

Lily's door was closed and had the 'Do Not Disturb!' sign on it. For half a moment Freya was tempted to leave

Lily be, remembering how she had felt at that age, but her sister's words were still ringing in her ears: 'You are the parent and you are in charge.' Gently she knocked on the door. For a split second there was silence, and then the boom of loud music. With a worried look in Daisy's direction, Freya pushed open the door. Lily was lying on her bed, doing something on her phone and taking no notice of her aunt whatsoever. Freya recognised the tactic. She walked over to the source of the music and turned it off.

'I think we need to talk.' She managed to bite off the end of the sentence, which would likely have been 'young lady', knowing full well that would not help the situation.

'I'm not talking to you. This is all your fault.'

Freya opened her mouth to argue but caught herself in time. 'Okay. You don't have to talk, but you do have to listen.' She leaned in and gently plucked the phone from her niece's hand. 'I'm sorry we were late today. I had to talk to Benji's teacher.'

Lily glared at her. 'Don't make it sound like it was nothing to do with you. You were late collecting Benji again, weren't you?'

Freya took a calming breath, remembering her customer service experience from her last Christmas job in a supermarket. 'Yes, you're right — I was. And I know I was late home to let you in too, and I'm sorry about that.' Lily rolled her eyes, but Freya thought that her niece might be thawing a bit. 'I'm going to work harder at getting everyone where they need to be, but I need something from you.'

She paused long enough to elicit a grumpy 'What?' from Lily.

'I need you to help me out here. I'm not used to being a mum and I'm not going to get it right. You're the oldest, and you could help me with the other two.'

'Whatever,' was Lily's response.

Freya could feel her anger building

and tried to push it down. 'It's up to you. Your choice. I'm going to do my bit; I just think it's time you did yours.'

'And if I do,' Lily said, eying her phone, 'can I have my phone back and go out this weekend? You know, if I'm going to have to help out, I ought to be rewarded. We wouldn't have to tell Mum.'

For about a heartbeat, Freya was tempted. If she agreed to Lily's demands, then she would have the help she needed, and might even have Lily on her side. But she knew deep down what Astrid would say about this arrangement. She turned Lily's phone over in her hand and then put it into the pocket of her jeans. 'No, I'm sorry, Lil. Your mum grounded you, and I'm not going to contradict her now.'

Lily made a noise and then threw herself onto her front, hiding her head under her pillow. 'It's all your stupid fault. If you weren't here with us in the first place, and always late, this would never have happened.' She might have her head buried in her pillow, but it didn't seem to stop her shouts carrying.

'I'm sorry you feel that way,' Freya said, using one of Astrid's favourite replies. 'And while I don't like what you've just said, I still love you.'

Freya stepped out of the room and closed the door. She leaned against it and shut her eyes. *If only Astrid could see me now*, she thought, *being all grown up and parental*.

Maybe she *could* do this after all.

Then the screaming started.

5

Freya bolted across the hall to Daisy's bedroom. The scream was high-pitched and panicked, not a yell of complaint but a scream of fear or pain. Freya was surprised that she could already tell the difference.

Daisy's bedroom was as she had recently left it when she kissed her niece good night, minus one thing — Daisy. Freya pulled back the duvet, knowing full well that Daisy couldn't possibly be hiding under there but needing to look anyway. She scanned the room. All the furniture was baby-sized, and there was no way that she could be hiding in the chest of drawers or the small wardrobe.

'Auntie Freya!'

Freya spun on the spot at the sound of Benji's voice, and she was out in the hallway and standing on the landing when Lily's door was yanked open.

'What's going on?' the girl asked, all trace of their earlier fight gone.

'I don't know, but Daisy's not in her bed.' Freya took the stairs two at a time, her heart beating hard and the taste of fear in her mouth. Something bad had happened, and it was her fault. She was in charge; she was the responsible adult.

She hit the ground floor and felt her knees jar; somehow her brain registered that there were more steps than there were. She held her hands out in front of her to prevent herself from colliding with the wall and used the momentum to spin round in the direction of a fresh round of screams, crashing into the lounge.

'Stuck, stuck, stuck!' yelled Daisy. She was running round in circles.

'What's stuck?' Freya said, torn between relief that there was no obvious blood gushing from wounds and the fear that something she couldn't see was worse.

38

Daisy continued to run around, hopping from foot to foot, rubbing her nose.

'She pushed one of Lily's beads up her nose!' Benji said as he ran round after his younger sister. 'I tried to get it out but it's too far up.'

'Why did she do that?' Freya wailed, looking between Benji and Lily, who both shrugged but continued to stare at their sister. Clearly none of them had any insight into the two-and-a-half-year-old's psyche.

'Daisy?' Freya grabbed the running child and lifted her up so that she could sit on the sofa with Daisy on her lap. 'Did you put a bead up your nose?'

Daisy seemed to freeze in place and then slowly shook her head. 'Uh-uh,' she said. 'Mummy said no beads.'

'You did, Daisy! I saw you!' Benji shouted. 'It went really far up because she sniffed really hard.'

'Let me see,' Freya said more softly to Daisy, who shook her head. When Freya reached out to tip her head,

Daisy sniffed once more. Then the wailing began.

'Ow, ow, ow!' Daisy shouted between sobs.

'We have to get it out!' Lily said, kneeling in front of Freya. 'Let me see, Daisy.'

Daisy shook her head firmly again. 'No, no, no . . . ' and then finally one more, 'NO!', shouted so loudly that Freya thought she might need medical attention for a burst eardrum.

'Even if we can see it, how will we get it out?' Freya asked the other two children, before remembering once more that she was supposed to be in charge. Both Lily and Benji looked as panicked as she felt. She took a deep breath. 'Right, you two — grab your coats and put your shoes on. I'll get Daisy's coat. Meet me at the front door in thirty seconds. No dawdling.'

'Where are we going?' Benji said, his voice wobbling, indicating that tears were on the horizon.

'To the hospital, dummy,' Lily said. 'How else are we going to get the bead out of her nose?'

In a split second, Benji had launched a punch at Lily's upper arm. Lily yowled and then grabbed Benji around the neck.

'Enough!' Freya yelled. 'Stop it, both of you.' The children opened their mouths to speak but Freya held up a hand, mimicking what she had seen Mr Barnes do in his office. 'I don't want to hear it,' she said firmly through gritted teeth. 'Your sister needs to see a doctor and she needs you to help me get her there. Shoes and coats, now!'

Freya juggled Daisy into one arm and pointed the other in the direction of the understairs cupboard. She thought Lily would argue, but Daisy chose that moment to start sobbing again, and that was all the encouragement Lily needed.

★ ★ ★

Freya and the children were directed to the part of the emergency department waiting room that had been designed for children. There were tired-looking posters on the wall and a grubby-looking plastic dolls' house in one corner. A basket of dog-eared books and toys that looked like they had seen better days had been discarded in the other corner. Freya had checked in with reception, and been directed to the rows of plastic seats that were welded to the floor and told to wait until they were called.

'How long will it be?' Benji asked, yawning.

Freya glanced at her watch. It was nearly eight o'clock. 'I don't know. As Daisy's so young, we shouldn't have to wait long.'

'The electronic sign says the waiting time's four hours,' Lily said, directing them all to the scrolling red dot matrix sign.

'I'm sure we won't have to wait that long,' Freya said, giving her a look that just made her shrug.

'Can I get a drink?' Lily asked.

'I'm hungry too,' Benji chimed in.

Freya was going to argue the point, but was suddenly overwhelmed with fatigue. She figured the fear and adrenaline were wearing off. 'Sure,' she said, feeling in her bag for her purse. 'Here. And Lily, sugar-free only.' She might be a parenting novice, but even Freya knew that sugary drinks this late in the day were a recipe for hyperactivity.

'Want Mama,' Daisy said sleepily.

'Me too,' Freya whispered, and wondered again if she should tell her sister now or wait until the issue was sorted.

Three hours later, all the kids were asleep. Freya held Daisy on her lap and Benji under one arm. Lily had curled up like a cat on the next seat along. The waiting room had grown silent, and Freya suspected that everyone was too bored or tired to speak. The only noise came when the electronic doors opened and closed and gave a glimpse of the organised chaos beyond.

'Daisy Morse?' a nurse in bright red scrubs called.

Freya stood, hoisting Daisy into her arms, and reached down to shake the other two children awake. After some complaints and confused 'Where are we?' questions, they all followed the nurse, who showed them into a cubicle with a long black trolley in it. Freya laid Daisy down on the bed and she turned over and continued to snore. The nurse pulled the curtain across.

'Mrs Morse, can you tell me what happened?'

'It's Miss Hardy, actually. I'm the children's aunt.'

'When Auntie Freya was upstairs fighting with Lily,' Benji said, 'Auntie Freya was late picking me from school, so we weren't at home when Lily got there, so Lily packed her suitcase and left home.' Benji paused for breath and seemed to finally realise that Freya was giving him the 'look'. He stopped talking and glanced at Lily.

'Stop talking, dumbo — you'll get Auntie Freya into trouble! Then who'll look after us?' Lily hissed. Benji's lip started to quiver, and his sister sighed before pulling him into a hug.

The nurse was not seeing the funny side of Benji's story, Freya thought; or perhaps he was right and there really wasn't a funny side to this particular story. 'I was upstairs talking to Lily, my other niece, when I heard a scream,' she explained. 'I came downstairs, and Benji told me that Daisy had pushed a bead up her nose.'

The nurse continued to look dead-pan. 'And what time was that?' he said, glancing down at the fob watch he had pinned to his uniform.

'About seven thirty.' The nurse looked at the little girl. 'Daisy was in bed, asleep.' Freya started talking quickly. 'I'd literally just checked on her. She was fast asleep, and then two minutes later she was downstairs pushing a bead up her nose. I've no idea why.'

She looked at the nurse, wondering if he had some answer, but he just said, 'Young children, particularly those of Daisy's age, can get into all sorts of trouble if they're left alone.' He put the emphasis on 'alone'.

Freya opened her mouth to defend herself, took one look at the expression on his face, and decided not to. What was the point? The man had clearly made up his mind about her, just like Mr Barnes.

'Do you have children?' Lily asked with an innocent air.

The nurse blushed and focused on the form he was filling in. 'The doctor will be with you shortly.'

'Thanks, Lil,' Freya said.

Lily shrugged in a 'no big deal' kind of way, but Freya was sure things between them had defrosted slightly. Apparently it was okay for Lily to be mad and mean to her aunt, but it wasn't okay for strangers.

The curtain was pulled back again and an older lady appeared, this time in green scrubs. She was wearing a badge that said 'Doctor Rachel', which was covered in tiny stickers. 'So, Daisy, have you been sticking things up your nose that are bigger than your elbow?' she asked, pointing to Daisy's elbow.

Daisy stared at her elbow, and Freya could see her trying to work out how you would get your elbow into your nose.

'Can I have a look?' the doctor asked.

Freya braced herself, expecting more hysterics, but Daisy just smiled and lay back, letting the doctor shine a light up her nose.

'Wow, that's pretty far up,' Doctor Rachel said with a smile. 'Have you been sniffing?' Daisy nodded. 'What do you think about me using my magic wand to get it out?' Doctor Rachel pulled out a pair of long-handled steel forceps. Daisy reached out a hand to her aunt and Freya squeezed it.

'Shall I tell you how?' Doctor Rachel

asked. Daisy nodded her head but her eyes were filling with tears. 'Well I put this bit up into your nose, and I say the magic words, and then out comes the bead!'

Now it was Freya's turn to look doubtful. Really? Surely it couldn't be that easy.

'But I need your help, Daisy. When I say 'now', I need you to say 'atichoo'! And the magic only works if you say it really loud. Can you say it really loud?'

Freya, Lily and Benji all answered at once: 'Oh yes!' They all laughed.

The doctor was true to her word and removed the bead in a few seconds. She gave each of the children a sticker and handed Freya an advice sheet on what to do if it happened again.

'Thank you so much,' Freya said. 'I've no idea why she decided to do it.'

The doctor smiled. 'Children are a mystery. One of the reasons I love my job!' And then she left.

By the time Freya had driven them all home, they were all asleep again.

Freya carried Daisy to bed, and Lily led a half-asleep Benji to his bed before falling in to hers. Freya was pretty sure she would be asleep before her head hit the pillow.

In what felt like only moments, her phone, which she had left in her pocket, was ringing. She pulled it out and stared at it, bleary-eyed. 'Benji's School' appeared under caller ID, and Freya's heart sank.

6

She continued to stare at it, wondering if she should just ignore it and ring them later to explain; but then the house phone started to ring and she knew she would have to answer it. She reached across to the bedside table and picked up the handset.

'Hello?' she said, trying to sound more awake than she felt.

'Is that Miss Hardy?' a familiar voice sounded. 'This is Mrs Jones. I have Mr Barnes on the line. He'd like to talk to you, dear.'

Freya swallowed and moved her head so she could see the clock on the other bedside cabinet. It read 10:05. She groaned. 'I'm in trouble again, aren't I?' she asked.

'Yes, Miss Hardy, I would say you are.' The voice at the other end of the phone was no longer the sympathetic tones of Mrs Jones, but the clipped, unimpressed, deep growl of Mr Barnes.

'I can explain. There's a very good reason why Benji's late,' Freya said, throwing the duvet off and sitting on the side of the bed.

'I think a quarter past ten is a little more than simply late, don't you?' Mr Barnes said, and Freya knew there was a disapproving look on his face even though she couldn't see him.

'Yes, well we didn't get into bed until nearly three this morning . . . '

'Miss Hardy, I hope I don't need to tell you that children need a suitable bedtime routine in order to be ready for a day's learning.'

'Mr Barnes, if you'd just let me finish,' Freya said, feeling herself getting cross at his manner, not to mention his assumption that she had simply let the children stay up until the early hours.

'Can I suggest we finish this conversation in person, when you bring Benji to school? Which I sincerely hope will be in the next half hour.'

Freya opened her mouth to speak but wasn't quite sure what to say.

'Excellent. I'll expect you both shortly.'

And then Freya heard the dial tone, which indicated that he had in fact hung up on her. She sat there for a moment staring at the phone. Who did this man think he was? He couldn't be more than five years older than her, but he was acting like he was a disapproving father! She had two more weeks of looking after the children, and there was no way she was going to be lectured by him every day.

There was nothing else for it. She was going to have to go and have it out with him, and find out exactly what his problem was with her. Freya was certain that it had to run deeper than Benji being late every day for a week, surely.

A quick glance at the clock told her she had managed to waste two precious minutes. If she was going to have that conversation with Mr Barnes, then they needed to be there within his ridiculous half-hour time slot. Freya ran out of the room and flung open Lily's door.

'Lily, we have to go. We're really, really late.'

The lump in the bed under the duvet didn't so much as stir. With a quick glimpse at the alarm clock on Lily's bedside table, Freya ran across the room and gave Lily a shake.

'*What?*' There was the teenager again.

'It's gone ten, Lily. We are so late!'

'Call school and tell them I'm sick.'

'That's a great plan,' Freya said, rolling her eyes, 'except you aren't actually sick. Now quick — wash your face and hands and get dressed.'

'But I've missed the bus,' Lily said, pulling the duvet back over her head.

Freya paused. That was a good point, and it wasn't like she had time to drive Lily to school and get Benji to his school in time for her meeting with Mr Barnes. How did Astrid do this?

'Help me get Daisy up and we'll

figure that out later.' Freya left the room, groans echoing in her ears.

'What's going on?' Benji asked, wiping the sleep from his eyes.

'We've overslept a bit, Benji. We need to get ready, and quickly.'

His eyes widened. 'Are we going to be late?' His little face crumpled, and Freya realised that despite all her best intentions, she had managed to let him down again. She knelt down in front of him.

'Just a little bit, but don't worry — I've spoken to Mr Barnes.' Benji looked doubtful. 'You aren't in trouble, Benji, I promise.' At least that much was true. Clearly it was Freya who was going to be summoned to the head teacher's office. 'Can you wash your face and hands and get dressed?' she asked before tearing back into her room and pulling on some clean clothes.

She ran a brush through her hair and tried not to glance at herself in the mirror. She looked exactly like what she was — someone who had just leapt out of bed and thrown some clothes on. Not exactly the look you were going for when you had to tackle a difficult conversation, but it would have to do.

She ran down the stairs and tipped some breakfast bars out onto the table, then got a couple of small bottles of water out of the fridge. She hadn't had a chance to make up Benji's packed lunch, but she would come home and do that and then drop it back in to Mrs Jones.

There was a clatter on the stairs and all three children appeared. 'Okay, everyone grab a breakfast bar and some water. We're going to have to eat on the way.'

'Benji can't go to school like that,' Lily said, pointing a finger at the school sweatshirt Benji was wearing. Freya could see that it had mud around the cuffs and a huge splodge of what appeared to be dried yoghurt down the front.

'Lily's right,' she agreed. 'Benji, go put a clean one on.'

'There wasn't one in my cupboard,' he said plaintively.

Freya frowned. They didn't have time for this. And then her eye spotted the overflowing laundry basket. She groaned inwardly. She had thought she could get away with saving the laundry until the weekend; had assumed that the clean uniform Lily and Benji had on Thursday would do for Friday. Clearly she was wrong. There seemed to be so many unwritten rules of parenthood that she wondered briefly if she should try and buy a book on the subject.

She pulled the other sweatshirt out from near the bottom of the pile and was nearly buried under a sea of dirty clothes. She held it up to the light. It wasn't exactly clean, but it was less grubby than the one her nephew was currently wearing. She handed it to him, and Lily wrinkled her nose. Freya gave her a warning look along the lines of, *Please don't say anything or you'll upset him and we'll never get to school.*

Benji pulled on the sweatshirt and Freya gave him an encouraging smile. Most boys wouldn't even have noticed or cared about the slightly dirty clothes, but Benji wasn't one of them. He cared a lot, possibly too much, about what other people — particularly the adults in his life — thought of him.

'Right, let's go,' Freya said, forcing some enthusiasm into her voice.

★   ★   ★

The nearer to school they got, the more she felt like dragging her heels. However much she tried to convince herself otherwise, she really didn't want to face Mr Barnes. Some of the earlier indignation had faded, and all she could really see was that he was probably right despite his haughty, judgemental tone.

When they walked through the school gates, which she had to open since they were closed during the school day, she could see him standing

57

outside the school entrance, arms folded, waiting for them. She wouldn't put it past him to be tapping his foot.

Benji stopped walking beside her, and even Lily looked a little fazed. 'Lily, can you play with Daisy for a few minutes?' Freya said. 'I need to have a quick word with Mr Barnes, and then I'll drive you into school.'

Lily stared at her but nodded and took over control of the pushchair. Freya reached out for Benji's hand and they both walked slowly towards Mr Barnes, each feeling a sense of impending doom.

7

Freya stood as Mr Barnes knocked on the door to Miss Parfect's room and then opened it. 'Miss Parfect, sorry to interrupt,' he said, and Freya was sure that it was for her benefit, 'but here's Benji.'

To Freya's relief, the young teacher smiled and held out a hand to the little boy. Freya could almost sense the tension falling from his shoulders as he headed into class.

'Bye, Auntie Freya,' he called with a distracted wave before throwing himself into the morning's activities.

'Miss Hardy,' Mr Barnes said, closing the door, 'perhaps you could follow me to the office. I appreciate you don't have much time to spare. Would I be right to assume that you're going to drop Lily into school?' His tone was so cool that Freya wondered if he breathed ice not fire.

'Yes, that's correct, so if we could keep it brief I'd appreciate it,' she said, trying to match his tone but knowing she was failing. She simply didn't have the practice in being judgemental and superior. Apparently, she thought, it took years of work.

This time when she entered Mr Barnes's office, she noted that all the children's chairs were neatly stacked in one corner and that a single adult chair was in front of the impressive desk.

'Please have a seat.'

Freya looked up sharply, wondering if he was making a joke. His face was carefully neutral, so she could only conclude that the man had no sense of humour, and she could never date a man who you couldn't have a laugh with. She felt some colour rise in her cheeks at the thought. Where had *that* come from? As if it would ever be a possibility in any universe!

'Since we're short of time, I won't offer you a coffee, but I'll get straight to the point. Benji cannot be late for school. It affects his learning, and you may not have noticed but it upsets him greatly.'

Freya clenched her hands in to fists and reminded herself to stay calm. She might not be parenting material, but she loved her nephew, and the last thing she would ever want to do was upset him. 'You don't need to tell me that,' she said through slightly clenched teeth. 'However, I should point out that a medical emergency resulted in a trip to the emergency room last night. The waiting time was excessive and so we didn't make it home until the early hours. I believe the school's lateness policy states that an unexpected emergency can be considered an acceptable reason for lateness.' She smiled inwardly. *Yes, Mr Barnes, I've read the policy*, she said to herself.

Mr Barnes, for his part, leaned back in his chair and appeared to be reassessing her. 'Indeed it does. And what was the nature of this medical emergency?' He said the last two words as if they were in quotation marks.

'Daisy, my youngest niece, managed to get an object stuck up her nose,' Freya said with all the dignity she could muster. It sounded ridiculous even to her. Mr Barnes raised an eyebrow, and if she didn't know better she would say he was trying not to laugh. 'I was unable to remove it, and so it was necessary to take Daisy to the hospital for the procedure.' She knew that she was sounding equally as pompous as the head teacher, but she couldn't seem to help herself.

'And was it necessary to take Benji and Lily with you?' Mr Barnes said as if he had thrown down a gauntlet of challenge.

'I could hardly leave them at home to fend for themselves, now, could I?' Freya said imperiously. She might not know much about parenting, but that she did know.

Mr Barnes continued to study her. 'And you didn't think to telephone someone who could have perhaps watched the two older children for you?'

Freya wondered if any moment he was going to hold up score cards on her decision-making, like they did on that dance show on TV. 'As you know, the children's mother is in London on jury service, and the children's father is serving in the army overseas. I'm new to the area, so just who do you think I could have called?' She felt slightly embarrassed that it had not even occurred to her to call anyone, but she was right — she had no local contacts in case of emergencies. She had lived in the village for precisely six days.

'I see. And Mrs Morse didn't leave you the details of anyone who could provide assistance?'

'No,' Freya said, crossing her fingers at another little white lie. Astrid had left her the address book, but Freya wasn't about to ring up a total stranger and tell them that Daisy had managed to shove a bead up her nose.

'Then might I make a suggestion?'

'Of course,' Freya said, while inside her head she was screaming, *No you may not, you pompous overbearing idiot!*

'Perhaps you should take my mobile phone number, in case of emergencies? Should a similar situation arise, I'd be happy to provide support.'

Freya could not have been more surprised if he had offered to take her out on a date. She wished she had a mirror to see the look on her face — a mixture of shock, surprise, and possibly a question mark. Was this man really offering to give her his phone number? She looked round her just to check that she was still in a head teacher's office and hadn't accidentally wandered into a speed-dating evening.

He added, 'Only if you feel it would help.' The words came out slightly hurriedly, and for the first time Freya felt Mr Barnes was slightly out of his comfort zone.

'That *would* be very helpful. If you

don't mind?' she said, trying to keep the smile from her face as she watched him busy himself with finding a business card to write on so that he didn't have to make eye contact with her. He scribbled on the back and handed it over. Freya took it with a smile, which seemed to make him squirm even more.

'Well, I won't keep you. You'll need to get Lily to school as soon as possible,' Mr Barnes said, seemingly back on form. He stood up as if to emphasise the point. Freya stood too, clutching the business card in one hand and returning the somewhat awkward handshake that he then offered.

'Miss Hardy?' Mr Barnes said as Freya was leaving the office. 'Please ensure that Benji's on time Monday morning.'

She nearly laughed. It seemed he had a powerful need to have the last word. Maybe that was a teacher thing. 'Of course, Mr Barnes. And if I have any problems over the weekend, I'll be sure to call you.' She turned and smiled sweetly into his slightly shocked face, then swept her way from the room.

Outside, Lily was running around after Daisy, who was laughing and squealing at being chased. It was a nice sight to see. Lily didn't seem to have the inclination to play with her younger siblings since she had started secondary school, and Freya knew that they missed it.

'How did it go?' Lily asked breathlessly, swinging Daisy round in front of her. 'Did you get a Mr Barnes lecture?'

'Sort of,' Freya said, feeling the business card in her hand. She had a sudden urge to share the events with Lily but quickly reminded herself that she was her eleven-year-old niece and not her best friend. 'Let's get back to the house, collect the car and get you to school.'

Freya ignored the moaning and groaning from Lily as she strapped Daisy back into the pushchair. She would call one of her friends later and see what they made of the mysterious Mr Barnes.

8

Having dropped Lily at school and been robbed blind — surely a school dinner couldn't actually cost ten pounds? — Freya and Daisy dashed back home, put a packed lunch together for Benji and, after a hurried phone call, met the lovely Mrs Jones at the school gates, who promised to hand it over to him without letting Mr Barnes know. With Daisy in her high chair happily crunching on carrot sticks and watching her favourite TV programme, Freya at last had the chance to make herself the cup of coffee that she had been dreaming about since the moment she'd woken up.

The fancy coffee machine was making all the right noises when her phone rang. She sighed; a moment's peace was really a thing of the past. She pulled the phone from her pocket and frowned slightly at the caller ID. It was

Astrid. Freya wondered if Mr Barnes had followed through on his threat and rung her sister. He wouldn't, would he? There was only one way to find out. She pressed the green telephone icon. 'Hi, sis,' she said.

There was a pause, and in an instant Freya knew something was wrong. For a heart-wrenching moment she thought she knew what. It must be Mike, Astrid's husband. 'Astrid, what is it?' she whispered, moving so that she could still see Daisy in her highchair but hoping the toddler was too wrapped up in magic ponies to pick up on the conversation.

No words were being spoken, but Freya knew that her sister was still there; she could hear the shuddering breathing. 'Astrid, you're scaring me. Please. Is it Mike?' She turned her back to the kitchen so that Daisy wouldn't hear.

'No, no, Mike's fine. I spoke to him last night.'

'Then what is it?' Freya asked, feeling

both relieved and confused. What could have made Astrid so upset?

'I've been called to a jury,' Astrid said, her voice still wobbly.

'Okay,' Freya said, still not getting it. 'You're on jury service, hon. That kind of comes with the territory.'

'You don't understand. It's a case at the Old Bailey. A fraud case.'

'Well that's going to be tedious,' Freya said, trying to inject some humour into the conversation, although she knew there was no way that Astrid was upset about that.

'Tedious and long, Freya. They're saying it could go on for months.'

Freya's legs started to shake and she found her way to the bottom step of the stairs. 'Months?' she said, knowing her voice had become high-pitched. 'But what about the children? Did you tell them about the kids?'

'Of course I did, Freya,' Astrid said, uncharacteristically cross. 'They asked about child care, and I said that my sister was looking after them for the next two weeks, and they seemed to think that settled it. They're going to pay you . . . ' Her voice trailed off.

Freya's mind was whirring and she struggled to figure out what to say next. 'Its fine, Astrid, really. I can stay and look after them. It's not like I have my tickets booked. Travelling can wait till you get back.' It wasn't exactly what she'd planned, but she couldn't bear to hear Astrid so upset and not do something about it.

'But I might not be able to come home every weekend. They're saying that because it's such a high-profile case, they might sequester the jury. I don't know how the kids will cope.' Astrid was crying now, and the words were pouring out of her. 'I don't mean that you won't take great care of them, because I know you will. But they find it so hard with their dad away for long stretches, and now me. I'm a terrible parent!' she wailed.

'Astrid, stop. You are an amazing parent and you know it. The children are very resilient, and they'll be fine.' Freya couldn't help but cross her fingers, warding off another white lie. The truth was that she had no idea how the children would react, and if they reacted badly she couldn't exactly blame them. The thought of Astrid being away for months made her want to curl up in a ball and cry herself, and she was an adult. 'And we can talk to you over the internet,' she carried on. 'We can do what Mike sometimes does, and you can read Daisy and Benji a bedtime story and do all the voices. And when you can get home, we'll make the most of the time.' Freya knew that she was babbling now. 'It'll be okay, Astrid. I promise I'll take good care of them.'

'I know you will; I'm not worried about that. You'll be fantastic.'

Freya winced a little, pretty certain that her performance so far could not be classified as fantastic.

'I just hate to be away from them for so long.' There was a noise in the background. 'Freya, I have to go. I'll try and call again tonight before Daisy goes to bed. I can tell them then — unless you can?' Her voice was almost pleading, and Freya knew she would never be able to say no.

'Of course I can,' she said firmly. 'No problem.'

'I think it might be better coming from you, and then I can talk to them about it a bit more later rather than shock them all in one go.'

After Astrid hung up, Freya sat on the stairs and stared at the wall. What on earth was she going to do? And more importantly, how on earth was she going to explain this to the children? She wouldn't blame any of them if they had a total meltdown. And she didn't blame Astrid for not wanting to tell them, as she would surely get upset, which would only make things worse. But still.

Freya sighed. It wasn't as if she even had anyone she could ask to come and help her. She thought about asking Jan,

Lily's friend's mum; but although she seemed friendly, it wasn't as if Freya knew her very well. The business card seemed to be burning a hole in her pocket, and for a brief moment she considered it. But it didn't last long. There was no way she was going to go to Mr Barnes for help. She would just have to manage on her own, just like Astrid had done every time Mike had been deployed. She could do this, couldn't she?

Operation Break News Gently swung into action. Freya knew what to do. She was going to cook the children's favourite dinner, the one thing they could all agree on: pizza. Followed by ice cream sundaes with all the trimmings. She glanced at her watch. If she was going to be at school to pick up Benji on time — and whatever else happened today, she was going to be there, and early to boot — then she needed to get a move on. She scooped up Daisy and headed for the supermarket to stock up on goodies.

She arrived at the school gates with twenty minutes to spare, trying not to feel too smug. She hoped that Mr Barnes would be out in the playground as usual and see her and Daisy casually waiting for Benji to come out of class.

By the time the old-fashioned bell sounded inside the school, the playground was swarming with parents and children. Benji was one of the last children out; and Freya had a sneaking suspicion, which filled her with guilt, that he thought there was no point in rushing since she was always late. She raised an arm and waved, calling his name. His surprised expression confirmed her worst fears, but the spreading grin squashed them back down. As did the sight of her nephew running towards her. She knelt down and threw her arms wide.

'You're here!' Benji shouted.

'I said I would be.' Her laugh died slightly when the look on his face told her that he didn't have much faith in her promises. 'Benji, I swear that from now on, I will be here on time to pick you up.' In reality, she admitted to herself that she could muddle through for a couple of weeks; but if she was going to be doing this for a couple of *months*, then she knew she would have to get to grips with the situation, and fast.

'Hi Daisy!' Benji said more cheerfully than he had sounded in days, and Freya wondered how long it would last.

'Miss Hardy,' a voice said.

Freya turned round, trying not to grin in an 'I told you so' kind of way. 'Mr Barnes,' she said.

He held out an arm to indicate that she should step away from the children, and she complied, all the while wondering what she could have possibly done this time.

'Miss Hardy, Mrs Morse has telephoned me and explained the situation.'

Freya shot a hurried glance in Benji's direction. This wasn't how she'd wanted him to find out, but Benji was dancing around the pushchair making Daisy laugh, and clearly wasn't paying attention.

'I appreciate that this wasn't planned, but I think we may need to speak about how you'll cope for the next few months.'

Freya shot him a warning look. This man really was unbelievable.

'I haven't spoken to Mrs Morse about any of the issues,' he said as if Freya should be grateful. 'But if you need any assistance, I think it would be in the best interests of the children if you called me.' He gave her a meaningful look, which she decided she should ignore in case she gave in to the desire to punch him.

'There's no need. We'll be fine,' she said pointedly. 'Goodbye, Mr Barnes.' She whirled around and started to wheel the pushchair across the playground. 'Come on, Benji,' she said loudly enough for Mr Barnes to hear. 'We have pizza for tea, your favourite. And we wouldn't want to be late to meet Lily from the bus.' And with that they headed off home, Freya more determined than ever to never ask for Mr Barnes's help, however bad things got.

9

It was only two hours later that Freya was seriously reconsidering her decision. The meal, as predicted, had gone down well, with everyone clearing their plate and no requests to get down or comments that they weren't hungry. Freya was just setting up the ice-cream factory, as it was known, laying out small bowls of sprinkles and chocolate drops, when she realised that Lily was staring at her with one hand on her hip.

'What's going on?' she asked in a suspicious tone. 'You've barely managed to reheat one of the meals Mum left in the freezer. What's with all this?'

'We'll talk about it later,' Freya said in what she hoped was a light-hearted voice, but still with enough edge that it would give Lily the heads-up.

'I think we should talk about it now,' Lily said firmly, and Benji stopped his attempt to stealthily help himself to the chocolate buttons, and stared at her.

Freya pulled a face at her niece, hoping she would get the message. She'd seen Astrid do it many times with the desired result; but either she herself didn't have the right technique, or Lily didn't care. Freya thought about arguing that they could talk about it later, but she knew that wouldn't help, as Benji would get more anxious and Lily more suspicious. She sighed. 'Okay, let's sit down,' she said. Daisy was in her highchair banging a spoon on the plastic shelf, and so Freya dished her up some ice cream to distract her.

'Is it Daddy?' Benji asked, his voice all wobble, and his eyes filled with tears. Freya could have kicked herself. She should have made it clear before that it was nothing like that. She reached out to squeeze his hand.

'No, Benji. Daddy's fine. He's going to talk to you over the weekend as usual.'

'Is it something to do with this stupid

jury thing?' Lily asked with her arms folded across her chest.

'Well it's not stupid, Lil. It's important.'

Lily's expression said 'whatever', and so Freya decided that now was not a good time for a public-service discussion. 'But you're right, it's to do with your mum and her jury service. You see, she's been asked to sit on a jury for a really important case.' Freya knew she was selling it wrong, since both children just stared at her, and she realised she needed to get on with it; rip the plaster off as quickly as possible. 'This case is going to go on for a bit longer than we all thought.'

'How long?' said Lily, who was leaning back in her chair as if it didn't really matter to her; but the tiny frown gave it away. She didn't want her mum away for longer any more than Benji did, with his screwed-up face showing he was trying not to cry.

'We're not really sure, but it could be months.' There, she had said it; she had told them. That was what parents did, wasn't it? You were brave enough to tell your children the tough things in life. But her sense of relief that she had done so was short-lived. Benji broke into loud sobbing wails, and Lily, in an unusual display of affection for her pre-teen years, pulled him onto her lap and enveloped him in a bear hug. Her baleful look at Freya told her in no uncertain terms that she had got it wrong, again.

'Mummy's going to be on the computer tonight, Benji, so you can talk to her and see her,' Freya said soothingly. 'She's going to try to get home when she can, when there's a break in the case.'

Benji's wails grew louder, and to Freya's dismay Daisy stopped eating her ice cream. The toddler's understanding of time wasn't exactly accurate, so Freya was pretty sure she hadn't really understood her words, though she could read the message Benji was giving out loud and clear. Her little face crumpled, and the air was ripped with another set of heart-wrenching cries. Freya went over and unbuckled Daisy from her seat and pulled her into her arms, and there they all sat, waiting for the crying to stop.

Nobody wanted to eat the ice cream and so Freya put it back in the freezer. She offered the children the opportunity to eat the other treats, but they just stared at her as if she had suggested they eat liver for their dinner. 'Look, I know you're upset,' she said, 'but your mum was very sad when I spoke to her, and I think we should try not to let her know that we're so sad too.'

Lily glared, but Benji seemed to be thinking about it.

'Benji, why don't you go and get ready for bed? I'm not sure what time Mummy will be on the computer, but I'll come and get you.'

He looked to Lily for confirmation, and to Freya's relief she nodded. Benji disappeared up the stairs.

'I'm going to need your help now more than ever, Lily,' Freya said. 'And before you say anything, I know it's not fair. It's not fair to any of us, but it is what it is, and we can't change it.' She continued to rock Daisy, who had fallen asleep in her arms, worn out with all the crying.

'If Mum's going to be away for that long, I'm going to go and stay at Steph's. Without me here, you should be all right with the other two.' She sounded like an adult making a reasonable suggestion, and Freya nearly fell for it.

'Lily, your mum's already made that decision, and I don't think bringing it up now will help the situation, do you?'

'But I have homework,' Lily said as if she was talking to Daisy. 'How am I going to get that done if I have to look after the kids all the time?'

'I didn't say it would be all the time, Lil. I just thought it would be easier for them if you were around a bit more. You know they love you, and I was thinking about you playing with them for a bit each day, not taking on their care. That's what I'm here for. And when the kids are in bed I can help you with your homework.'

Lily raised an eyebrow. 'What, like last time?' she said archly. 'I changed my answers for my maths homework and I got a D!'

'Okay, so maths isn't my strong point. But I can help you with the other subjects. If we need maths help, I'll find you someone who can tutor you or something.' Freya's mind unwillingly went to Mr Barnes.

'Who? Mr Barnes? You'd only be asking him because you have a massive crush on him. I'd rather get a D than watch you two get all lovey-dovey.' And with that, she pushed her chair away from the table so harshly that it tipped over with a crash.

Daisy woke with a start and then burst in to tears. Freya held her breath as Lily stomped upstairs, sounding like a baby elephant. Freya continued to rock Daisy, whose tears started to quieten as she fought her own. She was feeling sorry for herself, not to mention for the children and Astrid. She told herself firmly that she had two minutes to wallow and then she had to get a grip.

Her two minutes were up with Lily's announcement: 'Benji, Mum's on the computer!'

There followed stampeding feet and loud shouts of, 'Hello!' Freya shifted the sleeping Daisy in her arms so that she could carry her upstairs. She poked her head into Lily's bedroom and saw both kids lying on the bed, having an animated conversation with their mum about school. There were no signs of tears, which was a relief. Freya carried Daisy into her small box room and got her ready for bed, which the toddler managed to sleep through. When she went back into Lily's room, the children had just hung up.

'Right, Benji, time for bed. Go clean your teeth and find your book. We can read a couple of chapters before lights out.'

Benji's mood seemed to have lifted, and he bounced off the bed and out of the room. Freya sat on the edge of Lily's bed, which inexplicably seemed to annoy Lily for no reason that she could fathom. 'How're you doing, niece?'

'Fine,' Lily said, opening up her social media page on the computer.

'Lily, you know you aren't supposed to do that in your bedroom. Your mum's rules say you have to do that downstairs with an adult around, not to mention the fact that your mum said no computer time for a week.'

Lily groaned and pushed past Freya so that she could leave the room. Freya was pretty sure she heard her say 'whatever' as she passed.

'Mum says I can go and stay at Steph's, by the way. So I'm going.'

'Okay, well I need to talk to your mum about that later.'

'She said I could go now.'

Now Freya stood and walked over to her niece, reminding herself that she was in charge. 'I doubt that, Lily. How are you going to get there? Daisy is already in bed, and I can't leave her and Benji here while I take you. I'll talk to your mum later, and then if she's okay with it I'll talk to Jan in the morning.'

'She said I could go!' Lily said, her voice rising.

'If she did, then I'm also sure she said you'd have to wait till tomorrow. Now take the laptop downstairs.' Freya was impressed with her own firmness, and she hadn't even lost her temper.

Lily gave her one last sulky look and then marched out of the room. Freya sighed and wondered once more what had happened to her happy and loving niece.

She was halfway through chapter nine of *Science Adventures with Doctor Physics* when the sound of the front door slamming made her and Benji jump. They exchanged looks, and without a word Freya went running down the stairs.

10

She reached the front door in seconds and went to open it. It wouldn't budge, and it was then that she realised Lily must have locked it on her way out. Daisy had been able to open the front door for the last couple of months, so Astrid had taken to locking the door and leaving the keys on a high hook just by the coat rack.

Freya spun around and reached for the spare set of keys, but they weren't there — Lily must have taken them. Hissing with frustration, she searched for her bag, and finally found it buried under the children's school bags and coats, which had failed to make it to their rightful places on the named pegs.

With shaking fingers, she managed to unlock the door and yank it open. She ran down the front garden path to the pavement, looking right and left, but there was no sign of Lily. Freya suddenly felt eyes on her, and looking back to the house she could see Benji at his bedroom window looking down at her. She forced a smile onto her face and waved as she walked slowly back up the path. As much as she wanted to go and find Lily, she couldn't leave Benji and Daisy at home.

When she got back in the house, Benji was sitting on the bottom step of the stairs. 'Did Lily run away?' he asked.

'No, Benji. She just popped out to see Steph.'

'But she's not allowed to walk there on her own after dark; Mummy said so. And Lily said she was granted.'

Freya nodded. 'I think you mean grounded, Benji. And you're right, so she's going to be in trouble when she gets home. Now you go off to bed. I'm going to ring Steph's mum and ask her to bring Lily back.'

Benji nodded solemnly and then walked slowly upstairs. Freya reached for Astrid's phonebook and looked up Jan's number. 'Jan? It's Freya, Astrid's sister and Lily's aunt.'

'Oh hi, Freya. What can I do for you?'

Freya frowned and glanced at her watch. Surely Lily would be there by now. It couldn't be more than a ten-minute walk. 'Is Lily there?'

'Lily? No, she's not here. Is everything okay?'

Freya told herself to be calm. She realised that if it *was* a ten-minute walk, there was actually no way Lily could be there yet unless she had run all the way. 'Astrid's been called to a case that could take months. I had to tell the children this evening and they didn't take it very well. Lily said that her mum was happy for her to come and stay with you, but I haven't had a chance to talk to Astrid about it yet.'

There was a pause. Then: 'Lily would be welcome of course, but I haven't heard from Astrid either; and knowing her, I doubt she'd agree to something with Lily before speaking to me first.'

'My thoughts exactly. I'm sure this is just Lily acting out.'

'Do you want me to go out and look for her? My eldest is at home and he can watch the others.'

'I'm almost certain she's heading your way, so I think it'd be better if you wait at yours for her, if you don't mind?'

'Of course. I'll ring you as soon as she turns up and then I'll drive her straight back.'

'Thanks, Jan,' Freya said before hanging up, feeling more alone than she ever had in her life.

She tried Lily's phone, but the pop-song ringtone upstairs told her that her niece hadn't taken it with her. That was almost unthinkable, Lily without her phone, which told Freya that she'd had no real plan when she'd left. Freya could feel her panic start to build.

Ten minutes passed with her staring at her watch, and then another ten. No phone call from Jan. She sent her a text, but the reply was not what Freya wanted and needed to hear: 'No sign here.' Her niece had been missing for over twenty minutes. She knew there was only one thing she could do, short of calling the police . . . and that was to call Mr Barnes.

The phone rang and Freya wondered if he would answer. She also wondered what she would prefer, for about half a second, before she remembered that Lily was out somewhere and she had no idea where.

'Hello?' said a voice that was unmistakably his. Freya could also hear other voices and clinking glasses in the background. Mr Barnes, it seemed, was at the pub. She could feel herself colour up and had to swallow the lump that had suddenly formed in her throat, imagining what his reaction would be.

'Mr Barnes, this is Freya Hardy, Benji's aunt.'

'Hello, Freya,' he said, with no trace of his previous attitude.

'I need your help,' she managed to

say before the tears and the fear she had been holding back broke free.

'I'll be right there,' he said, and hung up.

Freya sat on the bottom step, hugging her phone and praying for it to ring with some good news. The gentle tap at the door was expected but still made her jump. From the size of the shadow she could see through the frosted glass, she knew it wasn't Lily.

She unlocked and opened the door. Mr Barnes seemed to study her face for only a moment before she found herself pulled into his arms. After a few moments had passed, he seemed to remember who he was and took an awkward step backward, seemingly to put some distance between them.

'What is it? What's wrong?' he asked quickly, clearly desperate to move things on, although whether it was through concern for what the situation might be or concern that he had just embarrassed himself, Freya wasn't sure. She took a steadying breath.

'It's Lily. She left when I was putting Benji to bed. We had an argument about her going over to her friend Steph's.' Mr Barnes nodded. Clearly he knew who Steph was. 'She locked me in the house, and by the time I found my keys there was no sign of her. I phoned Jan, Steph's mum, but she hasn't turned up there, and if she was going there then she should be there be now. She left her phone at home, and she's never without it, so I can't even call her.' She took another breath and willed herself to hold it together, although all she wanted in that moment was to be in Mr Barnes's arms and for him to say that it would be all right.

'Well there aren't many other places she could be. I'll head out and look for her.'

'Thank you, Mr Barnes.'

'It's Jamie,' he said with a small smile. 'Out of school, please call me Jamie. Let me have your number, and I'll call you as soon as I find her.' She told him and he typed it into his phone, then looked at her for a moment and disappeared out of the door.

Freya found her way back to the bottom step and sat down. She felt like she had been visited by a completely different man. Jamie didn't seem to bear any relation to the stuffy and pompous Mr Barnes, but her mind quickly pushed it aside as her thoughts returned to Lily. Mr Barnes would know where to look. Jamie would find her.

11

For what felt like the hundredth time Freya looked at her phone, as if she could have missed a call when she was sitting there with it in her hand. She had texted Jan to let her know what was going on, and Jan had texted back to say that she had spoken to Steph, who had sworn she had no idea where Lily was or what she was doing. She said that her daughter seemed genuinely upset and so was certain she was telling the truth.

The fact that Lily hadn't planned this excursion was both good and bad news, but all Freya could focus on was the bad. Where was she? If this continued for much longer, she knew she would have to phone Astrid, and she couldn't imagine the distress the news would cause, especially when her sister was so far from home and powerless to do anything.

Her fingers clicked the green phone icon and hovered over the number nine. Surely it was time to call the police. Jamie had been gone for at least fifteen minutes. She pressed the number once and then pressed it again. Her finger was poised over the last nine when her ringtone sounded. It was a mobile number she didn't have in her phone, but she had spent the last fifteen minutes memorising it.

'Jamie?'

'Freya, I've found Lily. She's safe. I'm bringing her back to you right now. We'll be there in about ten minutes.'

'Thank you,' Freya managed to say before she finally let all her emotions go and sat on the step and cried. Padded footsteps moved down the stairs and she hurried to dry her tears. 'Benji. What are you doing out of bed?' she said with a smile.

'Is Lily home?'

'She's on her way, kiddo.'

'Are you sad about Mummy too?' he

said before squeezing himself into the small gap on the step beside her.

'A little,' she said, 'but mostly I'm relieved that Lily's okay.' She felt a small hand slip into hers.

'Lily scares me sometimes too,' he said solemnly.

Freya smiled, suspecting that they were talking about similar situations.

'She shouts a lot these days.'

'I don't think she means it, Benji,' Freya said, giving his hand a squeeze and wondering if he was old enough for a talk on hormones and growing up.

'I wish she wouldn't, though.'

'Maybe you should tell her that.'

Benji nodded thoughtfully and then leaned into Freya, who lifted her arm and pulled him into a hug while they waited for Lily to come home.

When the knock on the door finally came and Freya opened it, it was clear that she wasn't the only one who had been crying. Lily's face was pale but streaked with tear tracks. Freya pulled her off the doorstep and into her arms, torn between wanting to berate her for being so foolish and hug her tightly. She wept with relief.

'I'm so glad you're safe,' she murmured into Lily's hair before taking a step back to allow Jamie into the house as well. 'But I'm so cross with you, too.'

'I'm sorry,' Lily managed to say between sobs. Freya continued to hug her until the sobbing subsided a little.

'I think it's time you were both in bed,' Jamie said, and it took Freya a moment to remember that he was still there. 'Perhaps it'd be better if you both slept on this and talked about it in the morning.'

It was a suggestion rather than his usual order, but it did rankle a little. However, Freya could see that Lily was worn out, and she knew that if she tried to have a conversation now, it would probably deteriorate into another shouting match. 'Mr Barnes is right,' she said, giving her niece a kiss goodnight. 'Off up to bed, both of you.

I'll be up to check on you in a few minutes.' She kissed Benji on the top of his head as he walked past, and she watched them both troop upstairs.

'I don't know about you, but I could do with a coffee — unless you have something stronger?' Jamie said, and he headed off towards the kitchen before Freya could formulate a response.

She stared after him, wondering how they had moved from cross words in his office to drinking together at her house. She shook her head. It really had been one of the strangest weeks ever. She followed him into the kitchen just as he was helping himself to two mugs from the mug tree.

'I have beer if you prefer.'

His eyes lit up, which told Freya the answer to that question. She pulled a bottle from the fridge for him and a half-full bottle of rosé for herself. Stepping around him, she found a glass, which gave her a few extra moments to decide what to say next.

'Thank you — for everything. It

sounded like I'd dragged you away from a night out.'

Jamie shrugged as he drank from his beer bottle. 'Just darts at the pub with a few mates, nothing important.'

Freya looked at him again, wondering how this Jamie and that Mr Barnes could be one and the same person. 'Well thank you anyway,' she said as she tried to figure out exactly who he was. 'I'm so glad Lily is safe. Where was she?'

'At the bus stop.'

Freya nearly choked on her wine. She had expected him to say at the local shop or at the playground. 'Why?'

'She'd decided she was going to see her mum.'

'In London? Did she even have enough money?' Freya felt suddenly like she needed to sit down, so she moved out of the kitchen and into the lounge before plonking herself down on one end of the sofa. Jamie sat down on the other end.

'She had some, but not enough to get

her beyond Garsby.'

Freya frowned as Jamie named the nearby town which had a train station. She shook her head. 'What was she thinking?'

'That's just it. She wasn't. It's not really her fault.'

Freya sat up a bit straighter, bristling at the perceived insult. Jamie seemed to notice, and as he laughed, she was momentarily distracted by the wide smile that seemed to transform his face.

'It's a scientific fact that teenagers' brains undergo a period of intense development that affects their ability to make rational decisions. I didn't mean to imply it was your fault.'

'That makes a change.' Freya clamped a hand over her mouth. She had not meant to say that out loud; it must be the adrenaline wearing off, or the wine. 'Sorry,' she said quickly.

'It's okay,' Jamie said in a tone that wasn't completely convincing. 'I take the welfare of my students very seriously.'

Freya bit her lip to stop herself from answering that she took the welfare of her nieces and nephew very seriously, too.

'What I mean,' he added, seeing her trying to hold in a retort, 'is that sometimes I can come across as a bit . . . '

'Officious?' Freya offered. 'Pompous, pushy, arrogant?' She was smiling now too.

'Well I wouldn't put it quite like that,' he said in his defence.

'Really? How would you put it?'

'Perhaps a little overzealous. Don't you need to check that the kids are in bed?' he asked with a mischievous look that told her he was blatantly trying to move the conversation back to her.

'As a matter of fact, I do,' she said serenely. 'I won't be a minute. Make yourself at home.' And she walked out of the room.

'All out for the count,' she said as she came back in a moment later.

Jamie was standing up and had

pulled his coat back on. 'I'd better go,' he said as if he had been waiting to say it the instant she came back.

'Okay,' Freya said, feeling like she'd missed something. 'You don't have to,' she added, and then immediately regretted it.

'I think I do.' He handed Freya his bottle of beer, which wasn't quite empty, and seconds later she heard the front door quietly close behind him. She put the bottle down and picked up her wine glass, trying once again to figure out what had just happened.

12

Freya had worked out that you didn't need an alarm clock at the weekend when you had small children. Benji was not easy to get out of bed on time in the week, but at the weekend he seemed to start bouncing around early. With a groan, Freya threw off the covers. She slipped her legs over the edge of the bed with a sigh and remembered what life was like when she could get up at the weekend when she wanted to.

The crashing from downstairs told her that Benji was likely trying to get breakfast for Daisy and himself, and Freya knew enough not to just leave them to it. She peeked into Lily's room, but the pre-teen-shaped lump told her that her niece was still asleep; either that, or she wasn't ready to face what happened yesterday, and Freya couldn't blame her. She felt like that herself.

As she walked into the kitchen, she had a flash of memory from the night before: Jamie — not Mr Barnes — asking for a beer, and being relaxed and friendly. Being, well . . . normal; and then Mr Barnes reappearing as he handed back his unfinished beer and excused himself in a hurry. What was that all about? She couldn't help but be curious, but reminded herself firmly that she was not looking for a relationship — and certainly not one with Mr Barnes.

'Morning, troops!' she said as her nephew froze in place. She laughed. 'It's okay, Benji. I just thought you might need a hand.'

'Mummy doesn't let us help ourselves, but I thought you might be tired after last night,' he said.

'Last night?' Freya queried, wondering how much the kids were aware of, but unsure why their possible knowledge that she'd had a drink with Mr Barnes should make her feel so guilty.

'You know, with Lily running away

and everything.'

Freya knew that Benji was studying her closely for a reaction, and it wasn't about Mr Barnes. Clearly five-year-olds didn't worry about their teachers dating their aunties. Not that it was a date, she told herself firmly. 'Lily's fine, Benji. In fact, she's still asleep.'

'But is she in trouble?'

'Well, she was already grounded with no computers, so I don't think much has changed, kiddo.' She smiled at Benji and he smiled back.

'Maybe she can play with us once she gets up. She builds great cars,' Benji said a little wistfully.

'Maybe,' Freya said, thinking that was about as likely as her marrying Mr Barnes. She shook her head to try and dislodge the thought. What was the matter with her? If she spoke any of these thoughts out loud to her friends, she was sure they'd tell her she was obsessed, and they knew what that meant: she fancied Mr Barnes.

Freya turned to switch on the kettle,

deciding that coffee might save her from this madness. She did *not* fancy Mr Barnes! He was arrogant and bossy. But Jamie, on the other hand . . .

'Poo-poo,' Daisy's voice piped up, and for quite possibly the first time ever Freya was glad to have a dirty nappy to distract her.

★   ★   ★

Two hours later, Freya knew they all needed to get out of the house.

'But I'm grounded,' Lily said sulkily.

'Well, your mum said you couldn't go out with your friends. She didn't say anything about house arrest, although if I told her about last night I suspect she'd pack you off to boarding school.' Freya was hoping that the outrageous suggestion would get a smile, but she got nothing but crossed arms and a pout. 'That was a joke, Lily,' she said just to be clear.

'It wasn't funny.'

'It wasn't that kind of . . . oh never

mind. Look, Benji and Daisy need some fresh air, and you and I need to have a chat.' Lily's frown deepened. 'Unless you'd rather talk to your mum about it.'

Lily's eyes widened in horror and she shook her head.

'In that case, go put some clothes on.' Freya couldn't help smiling to herself. Aunt 1, niece 0, for today at least.

The park was relatively quiet for a Saturday morning. Benji and Daisy ran off laughing and screaming while Freya found an empty bench. She patted the seat beside her and Lily reluctantly sat down. 'So . . . ' Freya said.

'I already said I was sorry.' Lily stared at her trainers as she scuffed them along the ground.

'I don't need an apology, Lil, but I do need to know what's going on. You really scared me last night.'

Lily shrugged and Freya waited, knowing that eventually her niece would feel the need to fill in the silence. She looked across the playground to see

Benji helping Daisy up the steps of the baby slide.

'It's just, sometimes . . . '

Freya could hear the frustration in Lily's voice, and it took her back to her own difficult time as a teenager. She reached out for the girl's hand.

'I miss Dad, and now Mum's away and is going to be away for ages. It's like they've abandoned us!' Lily blurted out, and then burst into tears.

Freya pulled her into a hug and kissed her. 'They love you very much, Lily. You know that.' She could feel the girl's body shake with a wave of sobs. 'Your dad's tour finishes in a couple of months, and hopefully your mum won't be away for long. And I'm here for you — you know that, right?' She pushed back her own feelings of inadequacy. This was about Lily, she told herself.

'I know,' her niece said, and it came out punctuated by sniffs. 'I just get so mad sometimes and I don't know why.'

Freya laughed now, and Lily looked at her quizzically. 'Welcome to the world of hormones, sweetheart.' Lily rolled her eyes, but Freya took that as a good sign. At least the crying had slowed. 'Trust me, hormones have a lot to answer for,' Freya said with a grin.

'Like you making cow eyes at Mr Barnes last night,' Lily retorted, and now it was Freya's turn to go wide-eyed.

'Lily, there's nothing going on between me and Mr Barnes,' Freya said in her most grown-up voice.

Lily stared at her until Freya had to look away. 'Yeah, right,' the girl muttered in the immortal words of teenagers everywhere. Then she ran off to play with her brother and sister.

Freya watched her go, and she had to admit that the score now stood at niece 1 and aunt 1. She tried to replay what had happened last night that would have given Lily the idea that she had a thing for Mr Barnes, but she really couldn't remember anything. It wasn't as if any of the children had been there when Jamie had hugged her. It was the sort of natural, spontaneous thing people did when someone was upset. It didn't mean anything. Her memory replayed the moment in slow motion, and she thought about how it had felt to be held and safe. Then, unbidden, her mind continued. What if Lily hadn't gone missing, and he had been holding her because he felt something for her? What would it feel like for his lips to kiss hers?

A shadow passed across her closed eyes, and she opened them and tried to remove any signs from her face of what she had been thinking of. She gave a sharp intake of breath when she realised it wasn't one of the children standing in front of her but someone much taller, who appeared to be holding something out to her. She shielded her eyes with a spare hand and the tall figure materialised.

'You looked lost in thought,' the voice said, and Freya tried her best to manage a mild smile that would give nothing away.

'Mr Barnes,' she said, trying to unclench her teeth from the embarrassment. 'What are you doing here?'

13

He held out a take-away coffee from the local coffee shop and Freya accepted it with a grateful smile — not just because she was desperate for coffee, but because it gave her something else to concentrate on rather than his smiling face.

'It's Jamie, remember? We aren't at school.' He flashed her that grin, and she had to momentarily close her eyes to give herself a chance to find her equilibrium.

'Thanks,' she said, raising the coffee cup. 'Jamie,' she added slowly. She was beginning to feel like Jamie and Mr Barnes were Dr Jekyll and Mr Hyde. Clearly today he had decided to be easygoing, friendly Jamie. Not to mention the fact that he hadn't explained why he was here. Surely any sane adult without children would not be up and about at this time on a weekend?

'How's Lily?' Jamie asked, looking at the children as they ran around shouting excitedly at each other.

'She's fine. She misses her dad. They're very close, and now with Astrid being away . . . ' Freya shrugged. She felt she didn't really need to explain the rest; surely it was obvious. 'It's a lot to cope with, as well as moving up to secondary school.'

Jamie nodded. 'Is she still struggling a bit with her maths?' he asked before taking a sip of his coffee.

Freya stared at him. She couldn't help it. He laughed. 'She was in my class last year,' he said by way of explanation.

Freya took at moment to think about this. It seemed to answer some of her questions.

'She's very bright, but numbers are not her thing. I did talk to Mrs Morse about getting her a maths tutor.' He turned to look at her. 'I can suggest a couple of people — unless you have it covered?'

Freya blushed. 'I'm a History of Art graduate. Alas, I suspect Lily's maths issues come from our side of the family.'

She was pretty sure that Jamie was hastily readjusting what he thought he knew about her; and while she would never admit it to anybody, she had to confess that she was pleased about that. She had no idea what he really thought about her — ditzy and useless, probably — but there was a lot more to her than her parenting skills, or lack thereof, and it did him no harm to know that.

'Really? There's a little art gallery in Garsby. Have you ever been?' He said the words, but his eyes were fixed on the children as if he wasn't ready to see her reaction.

'No,' Freya said carefully. 'It's on the to-do list, but I doubt I'll get round to it now.' She stared at his profile, trying to figure out what was going on. Was this the same man who had practically run out of the house last night?

'It's not on the scale you'd be used to in London, but they have some local artists whose work you wouldn't get to see anywhere else.'

Freya waited, and he seemed to risk a glance in her direction. He looked away quickly, but she saw a flash of something on his face. Maybe it was anxiety at what her response would be. 'Well I'd like to go, but I don't suppose they're that keen on having toddlers crashing around.' She gestured in the direction of Daisy, who was squealing as Lily pushed her on the baby swings.

'Perhaps you could get a babysitter?'

He said it so quietly that Freya wondered if her imagination was running away with her again. She frowned. 'But last night . . . ' she started to say, and then had the sudden sense that someone was glaring at her. She looked up quickly to see that Lily had stopped pushing Daisy on the swing and was in her familiar position of hands on hips, but this time she looked like a disapproving parent.

Freya stood up quickly as Lily shook her head before giving in to the demands of her sister to push her higher. 'Like you said last night, it's probably not a good idea.' She walked away quickly before she could change her mind, trying to work out if Lily had interrupted something Freya would like to happen, or if her niece had prevented a disaster that would only complicate things.

'Hey, Benji — I think it's time we went home. One more go.'

He nodded and then ran to the rungs of the steps that led up to the tallest slide. Freya risked a glance in Jamie's direction, but he was retreating in the direction of the village. He was walking with his back straight and shoulders square, and Freya felt sure that Mr Barnes was back. She didn't really have the time or energy to work out if she was upset about that. She had three children who were going to be without their parents for at least a couple of months, and she needed all her focus on them. Not to mention the fact that she was supposed to be saving and planning for her trip of a lifetime.

'Lily, Daisy! Time to go home, girls.'

'As long as we aren't dragging you away from your date,' Lily said softly. 'You could've told me you just wanted to come to the park so you could meet your *boyfriend*.' She had Daisy in her arms but still managed to perfect the stroppy teenager look.

'For the last time, Lily, Mr Barnes is *not* my boyfriend.' Freya could say this now, as she was absolutely certain that her recent rejection would put an end to Jamie and they would only see Mr Barnes from now on. 'I had no idea he was going to be here,' she added firmly. Her insides lurched at the idea of only seeing Mr Barnes from now on, but she ignored them. Her gut instinct had got her into plenty of trouble before, so it seemed a good time to start ignoring it. 'Let's go,' she shouted to Benji, and the little family headed towards home.

Once they reached their road, a big red van could be seen parked outside. 'The postman!' Benji said with the enthusiasm that came from never having received any kind of bill or bank statement. He started to jog along ahead of them. 'He's going to our front door!' he shouted over his shoulder before breaking into a run.

Freya could see that Lily's face had moved from practised disinterest to mildly intrigued.

'It's a parcel, and it has our names on it!' Benji shouted, and now he was jumping up and down. Freya scooped Daisy up into her arms and hurried towards her nephew, who she doubted could contain himself much longer. The postman had carried a large brown cardboard box up to the doorstep. As she approached, he handed her an electronic pad to sign, which she did. Glancing at the address, she instantly recognised her sister's handwriting.

'Let's get this inside so we can open it,' she said, and the children hurried in after her. There was a momentary scrabble as to who was going to open it, which failed when all three children realised they weren't going to be able to get into the parcel without the help of scissors.

Freya held a pair aloft in her hands. 'Okay, you three, I'll open the outer package and then you can go for it.'

Benji and Daisy hopped around as Freya cut through the thick packaging tape. As she cut through the last strip, the children, including Lily, surged forward. Benji was first in the box, and he pulled out a gift in dinosaur wrapping paper. He squealed with delight and proceeded to tear off the wrapping. Lily had pulled out a pile of books that Freya recognised as the girl's favourite due to the sparkly covers. Daisy's present was also wrapped, and Freya helped her uncover the surprise, which was a selection of plastic animals to swell the ranks of her toy zoo.

'I have a note from your mum,' Freya said, sparking a mild amount of interest. 'Kids,' she read, 'since you have been so fantastically well-behaved for Auntie Freya . . . ' She paused and tried to fight the smile on her lips. Lily's eyes were focused on the pile of books in her lap, but she at least had the decency to blush. ' . . . I thought a few treats were in order,' Freya continued. 'I hope you like them. And I hope you know how much I love you all. Be good for Auntie Freya. Love you to the moon and back, Mum.'

Freya looked up to see that Daisy was trundling over to her zoo, which was set up in the corner of the living room. Benji was pulling on a bright green dinosaur costume. Only Lily was paying her any attention. Freya smiled at her and thought for a moment that her niece was going to say something, but instead she stood up, her arms full of books.

'Do you mind if I go upstairs and read?' she asked so politely that Freya was reminded of her niece in younger years. 'I've been waiting ages for these.'

She looked at her sister. 'Or I could play with Daisy while you make lunch?'

Freya's smile widened. There may not have been an 'I'm sorry' in there, but it was definitely a peace offering. 'We'll be fine,' she said, nodding towards the stairs. 'Go start your books. I'll call you when lunch is ready.'

She watched her niece walk away and sighed with relief. Maybe they were all going to make it through this.

14

'Benji, you can't wear that to school. I've already asked you twice. Please go and put on your uniform.'

'We're going to be late,' Lily said. 'I'll miss my bus again.' While relations between her and Freya had thawed over the weekend, Lily was not unaffected by the Monday morning glooms, and they were on full display.

'We're *not* going to be late,' Freya said, trying to wrestle Daisy into her coat. 'Benji, I'm going to count to five, and if you aren't up those stairs and getting into your uniform when I'm done, you'll have to go to school dressed like that.'

When she looked up, Benji was standing there with his arms crossed. Clearly he had been taking lessons from Lily. 'Mummy brought it for me,' he said, as if that explained it all. Freya could detect a slight lip wobble and knew that if tears followed, they would definitely be late.

'But I don't think she meant you to wear it to school, Benji. What will your teacher say?' And in her head she couldn't help wondering what Mr Barnes would say. If they hurried, she must just get everyone where they needed to be before the bell rang. But since Benji was breaking a school rule, she doubted she would win any points for her parenting skills today.

'Benji, if you make me miss my bus again, you're going to be in big trouble,' Lily said angrily. Benji shoved her; and despite the fact she was quite a bit taller than him, she nearly fell over. Freya stepped between them.

'Enough, both of you! You know very well that we don't do any kind of fighting in this house.' Lily opened her mouth to argue, but Freya held up her hand and gave her the 'look'. 'Benji, get your school bag. You can go to school like that, but I will be telling your teacher that I told you to change into your uniform.'

He looked uncertain for a minute, and Freya wondered if he would bolt upstairs and change, which was not necessarily good news since then they would be late. Lily stuck her tongue out at him, and that seemed to do the trick; he slung his cartoon-hero rucksack over one shoulder and stood by the front door.

Freya sighed, not entirely sure that she had won the latest skirmish. 'Okay, let's go.'

They made it to the school bus stop just as the last student got on board. Steph appeared to have saved Lily a seat, which seemed to mollify her a little. They all stood and waved her off, and were rewarded with much eye-rolling from Lily and some pointing and laughing from the other students.

'Right, off we go,' Freya said, heading off up the hill towards the primary school.

'I think I should go home and

change,' Benji said, and Freya realised that he hadn't moved from his spot. 'I think maybe you're right. Mummy would want me to wear my school uniform.'

'Benji, we don't have time. If we go home now you'll be late again, and that can't happen, buddy. I told you all this back at the house and you said you wanted to wear that.' She gestured at his tail, which was dragging along the ground. But he didn't move even when she held out her hand for him to hold. 'Benji, come on, please.'

But again he stayed where he was, and so Freya turned around and started to push Daisy in her pushchair up the hill. She had seen Astrid use this technique before but it made her nervous, walking away and leaving him like that. She repeated over and over in her head that she was the adult and she couldn't give in to tantrums from small people, but it didn't really help, as she could feel the gap between herself and Benji widen. She gritted her teeth and kept walking, and it paid off. After what felt like forever, she heard the tell-tale thud of his feet and the accompanying swish of his tail as he jogged to catch up.

'Am I going to get in trouble?' he asked.

'I'm not sure, but what do you think your mummy would say?'

'Something about conversations?'

Freya frowned, wracking her brains for what Astrid might have said. 'Ah, I think you mean consequences — and yes, you're right. I gave you the option to change but you said no, so you might get in trouble for that.'

She glanced down at Benji, and seeing his crumpled face, wondered how Astrid did it. All she wanted to do right now was make everything better and take away Benji's sadness, but she knew she probably shouldn't. Astrid's words of advice rang in her ears: 'You have to let them make mistakes sometimes, sis. Otherwise how will they learn?' It had made perfect sense at the time, but putting it in to practice was harder than she thought.

She reached out for Benji's little hand, which gripped hers tightly. 'How about I walk you to your classroom today? Then we can talk to Miss Parfect together.' Freya knew she probably shouldn't, but maybe the news that Astrid was going to be away for longer than planned could be considered a reasonable excuse.

They crossed the playground together. A few parents drifted across after having dropped their children off, but most had already left for work or home.

'Miss Hardy, I'm afraid Benjamin can't wear a costume to school. I would have thought Mrs Morse would have explained that to you.'

Freya stopped short in front of a woman about her sister's age who was dressed in an eccentric getup of a long flowing tie-dyed skirt, a faded jumper and rows of beads. *You can talk*, Freya thought, but kept her mouth firmly shut.

'And Benjamin, I know that you know the school rules.'

Benji shrunk behind Freya's legs and she could feel herself bristle. Standing in front of her was the worst kind of teacher, in Freya's mind. The kind that never asked for an explanation and went straight in for punishment without even listening.

'I'm afraid Benjamin will have to spend the day in the time-out room.'

Freya didn't really know what that was, but it sounded bad, and she could hear Benji whimpering. 'I've never been in time-out,' he said, and Freya could hear his voice wobble with the upset.

'Well, you've never done anything this naughty before.'

Freya knew that she had now reached her limit. 'With respect, Mrs — '

'Caulfield. I'm afraid this is not open to debate. It does Benjamin no favours to hear his *guardian* arguing with an authority figure.'

'Mrs Caulfield, Benji's had a difficult few days, as I expect you're aware. I think what he needs right now is to get to class and have a normal day. I'll go straight home and bring his uniform in so he can get changed during first break.'

'No, I'm afraid that won't do. That won't teach him anything.'

'Then I'm afraid we have a problem, Mrs Caulfield. I believe there are extenuating circumstances around Benji today, and I've suggested a solution. I will not leave my nephew here if you're going to isolate him from his class and friends.' Freya could feel icy cold anger build inside her. There was no way she was going to leave Benji with this woman. Yes, he needed to learn about consequences, but not like this. She had always felt protective of her nieces and nephews, and right now she knew that she would do anything to keep them from any type of harm, even if it was merely an overzealous teacher.

'Then we'll have to go and speak to the head teacher,' Mrs Caulfield said, drawing herself up to her full height as if she thought a straight back would assert her authority more.

'Very well,' Freya said, gripping hold of Benji's hand. 'I suggest you lead the way.'

'If you insist. But you must realise, Miss Hardy, that you're wasting your time. Mr Barnes always supports his teachers — always,' she said ominously.

Freya followed behind her. She had hoped to avoid meeting Mr Barnes again, especially after the events of the weekend; but there was no way she was going to give in to this woman's bullying tactics just to avoid another confrontation with Jamie Barnes.

15

'Mr Barnes, I'm afraid we have a problem,' Mrs Caulfield said, sweeping into the head teacher's office.

Mr Barnes was juggling a cup of coffee and a pile of children's workbooks and looked like he was in a hurry. 'And what would that be, Mrs Caulfield?' he said as his eyes moved from her stern face to the sight of Benji in his dinosaur outfit and Freya, who was gripping her nephew's hand.

'I think you can plainly see what the issue is,' Mrs Caulfield said imperiously in a manner that made Freya's hackles rise.

Mr Barnes, to her surprise, merely raised a cool eyebrow before putting down his coffee cup and pile of workbooks. He walked around the desk and crouched down in front of Benji, who shrank back against Freya's legs.

'Morning, Benji. That's rather an unusual outfit for a school day, isn't it?' He said the words softly, and Freya felt Benji's tight grip of her hand loosen a little.

'Mummy sent it for me,' Benji said, and Freya glared at Mrs Caulfield as she snorted in response.

'Ah, I see,' Mr Barnes said, exchanging an understanding glance with Freya, who risked a small smile in relief at his reaction. 'Do you think she meant you to wear it to school?' he asked, his attention back on Benji.

The little boy looked down and scuffed his feet, making his tail swing back and forth. 'No,' he mumbled.

'Everyone wears their uniform to school,' Mr Barnes said gently.

'That's what Auntie Freya said.' He looked up at Mr Barnes. Some of the fear melted from his face as he saw that the head teacher was smiling at him.

'I don't see that it matters *why* Benjamin's wearing it,' Mrs Caulfield said with her arms crossed. 'The fact remains that he is, which is breaking a school rule, and so he'll need to spend the day in time-out.'

Freya watched as a silent conversation occurred between Mr Barnes and Mrs Caulfield. Benji had once again shrunk back so that he was hiding behind her legs, and she again told herself that she was not going to let him be put in isolation all day.

'I don't think that will be necessary, Mrs Caulfield,' Mr Barnes finally said. 'I think Benji understands that he needs to wear uniform to school. Don't you, Benji?'

Freya felt her nephew move, and when she looked down she could see his head nodding solemnly.

'Then I think the point's been made, Mrs Caulfield. But thank you for bringing this matter to my attention.'

Freya's mouth fell open. This was not what she was expecting at all. She had thought that Mr Barnes would be a stickler for rules — and even if he wasn't, that he would fulfil Mrs

Caulfield's prediction and support his staff on any and all occasions. She watched as Mrs Caulfield's face showed first shock and then disapproval. Mr Barnes held out an arm in the direction of the door, and it was clear to everyone that she had been dismissed. With a sniff and her head in the air, she left the room.

'Right — Benji and I need to get to class,' Mr Barnes said, heading back to his desk to retrieve his cup and pile of books.

'I was going to go back home and collect his uniform,' Freya said. 'I can be back here before first break.' She waited for Mr Barnes to look at her and tried to convey how grateful she was without using words. He seemed to consider the look, and then smiled in such a way that his whole face lit up.

'That might be an idea, Miss Hardy. I think the other children might be distracted by what's quite possibly the best dinosaur outfit I've ever seen.' He looked down at Benji. 'In fact, to be honest, when Mrs Caulfield brought you in I thought we had a real dinosaur loose in the school.'

Benji giggled and Freya joined him. It was good to hear him laugh. 'Daisy and I will be right back, Mr Barnes. I'll leave Benji's uniform with Mrs Jones.'

'That sounds perfect,' he said before gesturing for Benji to follow him. 'I'll take you to your classroom and explain to Miss Parfect about the little mix-up with clothes this morning.'

'Thank you,' Freya said to Mr Barnes's retreating back. She waited, hoping he would look back, and she was rewarded as he smiled at her again. She felt that she'd just caught a glimpse of the real Jamie.

★　★　★

At the end of the school day Freya was waiting for Benji to come out of class, as she had promised both him and herself that she wasn't going to be late again. Her nephew came charging out with the sea of other children. Freya was pleased to see he was back in his uniform, with his dinosaur costume slung over his shoulder. He also had a white sheet of paper in his hand. He ran up and handed it over.

'I have to give you this — it's very important,' he said as he used his spare hand to scratch at his head. Around her, Freya could hear the parents groaning, and muffled conversations along the lines of, 'Not again!' She smoothed out the piece of paper and read the news that was causing such a stir. She didn't have to read too many lines before she felt like she, too, needed to scratch her head.

'Head lice?' she said in horror.

Benji just shrugged and continued to scratch at his head.

'Better get to the chemist quick,' a mother said behind her. 'Since there's only one, there'll be a rush on the stuff that doesn't smell so bad.'

Freya nodded distractedly as she read

the rest of the letter. Basically she would need to treat the whole family, including herself, which set off another wave of intense itchiness; but this time she felt like it was affecting every part of her, not just her head.

'Great,' she said gloomily. 'Come on, Benji. We'll go meet Lily from the bus and then head to the chemist.

* * *

Two hours later they were all sitting around the bathroom with wet hair that smelt so strongly of chemicals that Freya was sure her eyes would start to water.

'Why didn't you get the non-smelly stuff?' Lily said irritably. 'You can get a spray that smells okay and doesn't make you stink of it for days.'

Freya sighed. 'By the time we picked you up from the bus, the chemist had sold out of that. And besides, this is the best way to treat head lice if you actually find it.' She said this in a whisper as she tilted her head towards Benji.

'Typical!' Lily said. 'Typical disgusting boy who never has a shower.' She made a face at Benji, who went a little red.

'Auntie Freya said they only like clean hair, so if you haven't got them, *you* must be the yucky one!'

Freya moved between them. 'Enough! Lily, comb through Daisy's hair while I do Benji's. We have to leave this in overnight, so I've put a towel on everyone's pillow.' Freya shuddered; she couldn't help it. Lily wasn't wrong — it was all pretty disgusting.

When she texted Astrid, she was informed that it was the third time that year the children had had that particularly unwelcome visitor, which didn't do much to improve Freya's mood, particularly with the rather ominous prediction that there were worse childhood illnesses than head lice.

The next morning, despite several shampoos each, they still all smelt like a walking chemist's shop.

'You know, there's only one thing worse than actually having head lice,' Lily said as she pushed last night's homework into her school bag. 'It's *smelling* like you have head lice.' She paused and sniffed at a strand of hair for what had to be the hundredth time that morning.

Freya was trying to get Daisy to eat her breakfast, but she too seemed to be affected by the dismal mood and kept pushing the bowl away, and in a final act of defiance threw her spoon on the floor. The crash seemed to momentarily distract Lily, who had just started on all the reasons she needed to stay home from school until her hair smelt 'normal'. She walked over to her sister and placed an experienced hand on her forehead. She raised an eyebrow at Freya, who was a little mystified until she, too, felt Daisy's forehead, which was red hot.

Lily pulled a thin plastic tube from one of the top cupboards and expertly popped it under Daisy's arm. The beep told them both that Daisy had a temperature of thirty-eight degrees.

16

'She'll need some paracetamol,' Lily said before walking out to the hall to pull on her school shoes.

Freya had to stand on tiptoe to reach the medicine cupboard. She pulled out the box of tablets, wondering how on earth she was going to get Daisy to swallow one. She herself could barely manage it, and she had bad memories of her mum giving her crushed tablets in a teaspoonful of jam. With a shrug, she searched the fridge until she found the strawberry jam.

'What're you doing?' Lily said in her most disparaging tone.

Freya waved the box at her. 'Giving Daisy paracetamol. She has a temperature, remember?'

'What do you need the jam for? It's already strawberry-flavoured.'

Freya looked again at the box. Lily

made an exaggerated 'I'm surrounded by fools' gesture and pulled out a bottle of pink liquid from the medicine cupboard. 'This,' she said, handing the bottle to Freya, 'is for children. And this,' she said, taking the box off of Freya and putting it back in the cupboard, 'is for grown-ups.'

Despite the attitude that was coming off of Lily in waves, Freya couldn't help but blush. She really ought to know this kind of thing if she was going to be left in charge of small people.

'There's a syringe in the cutlery drawer,' Lily said.

Freya just stared. What was so great about medicine for children if it meant you had to inject them with it? Surely that was worse than taking a teaspoon of disgusting medicine with jam. Lily waited, arms crossed, but Freya didn't move, and so Lily sighed and pulled a plastic tube from the drawer. Taking the bottle from Freya, she deftly filled the plastic tube and then walked over to Daisy.

'Hey Daisy, I have some magic medicine for you.' Daisy obediently opened her mouth and Lily squirted in the bright pink medicine. 'Maybe I should stay at home to take care of Daisy,' Lily said a little hopefully.

'Nice try, niece of mine, but now you've shown me the ropes I think I can manage.'

Three hours later, Freya was less sure. Daisy was in turns grumpy and then sleepy, and she couldn't seem to sit still. She was scratching herself, but Freya was fairly confident that the head lice issue was gone for now. She was at a loss; none of her normal tricks were working for very long. It was a relief when her phone went.

'Astrid — you must be psychic or something!'

'Why, what's wrong?'

'Daisy's got a temperature and she won't settle. She seems itchy, but I followed the instructions on the head lice treatment so I don't think it can be that.'

'Have you checked her for a rash?'

'A rash?' Freya echoed, feeling her heart drop even lower than it had at the head lice letter.

'Just lift up the front of her top and have a look. Anything?'

Freya peered closely as Daisy tried to wriggle away. 'It looks like a couple of blisters. Do you think she's allergic to the head lice stuff?' She now felt guilty and worried. What if this was all her fault? 'I mean we put it on in the bath, but I was careful to use a towel to catch the drips.'

'What did you use?'

Freya told her and could almost see her sister shaking her head. 'I've used that before so it's not that. Hang up and send me a photo.'

Freya did as she was told and waited for the phone to ring back.

'I hate to break this to you, Freya, but Daisy has chickenpox.'

Freya closed her eyes momentarily and tried to imagine that her sister had said something else. 'Right,' she said finally. 'So should I take her to the doctor?'

'No, they won't do anything. I'm sure that's what it is. I've seen it before, and I have all the supplies you need in the medical cupboard. There's some special bath stuff and then some calamine lotion. You need to dab that on each spot with some cotton wool. The most important thing is not to let Daisy scratch.'

Daisy was now rubbing her back against the corner of the wall, so Freya hurried over and picked her up, cradling the phone between her chin and her shoulder. 'And how exactly do I do that?'

'Mittens,' Astrid said as if it were the most obvious thing in the world. 'There's a set of those in the medicine cupboard too. I got them just in case.'

'You knew this was going to happen?' Freya asked incredulously.

'Did I suspect that my children would succumb to a common childhood illness? Yes, Freya, I did. That's what mothers do. We prepare for the worst to happen because sometimes it does.'

'Wait a minute — you said 'children'. Only Daisy is sick.'

'The good news is that Lily will be fine; she had it before Benji was born.'

'And what's the bad news?' Freya asked, although she was pretty sure she already knew the answer.

'Benji's never had it.'

Freya leaned against the wall with Daisy in her arms. The little girl appeared to be in a tired phase and was snuggling into her chest. 'Do I even need to ask what the chances are that he'll get it?'

There was silence from the other end. Then: 'I'll tell the judge. Maybe he'll let me come home.'

'Astrid, you said that they'd only release you if there was a dire medical emergency, and I'm pretty sure they aren't going to think that a case of chickenpox is exactly dire.' Freya paused. 'Is it?' Now she stood up straight and looked at Daisy, wondering if she should be rushing her to the hospital.

'Calm down, Freya. Daisy will be fine. Regular paracetamol for her fever, and baths and calamine for the itch. She'll be tired and grumpy but that's about it.'

Freya sighed with relief. 'Well then you need to relax, because that much I'm sure I can manage.'

There was more silence from the other end of the phone.

'Why do I get the feeling that there's more bad news?'

'The things is, Freya, I'm pretty sure *you* never had it.'

'So? It's a childhood illness. I'm not likely to get it now, am I?' She waited for her sister to tell her that she was just fooling around, like a form of parenting hazing, but there was nothing. 'Oh come on. If it's so common, I'm bound to have had it.'

'Freya, I practically raised you, and I'm pretty sure you didn't.'

'In that case, Daisy and Benji will have some company in the itchy/grumpy stakes.'

'Freya, I'm so sorry.'

Freya walked over to the sofa and eased herself down. Daisy had fallen asleep in her arms and stirred a little at the movement. 'It's not your fault, Astrid. Kids get sick; that's one of the many joyous things about them.' She kept her voice light-hearted, but she couldn't completely ignore the feelings of doom that were welling up inside.

'You have to promise to tell me if you get sick. Then I'll go to the judge and demand to be released. I'm not a prisoner — it's not like I did anything wrong!' Astrid's voice was getting shriller with every word, which was a sure sign she was starting to lose it.

'Hey, I thought I was the doom-and-gloom merchant and you were Mrs Positive!' This at least got Astrid to stop breathing like she was running. 'At the moment only Daisy is sick. Who knows, maybe Benji won't get it.' She paused and knew that Astrid was about to launch into another speech. 'And even if he does, I'll cope fine. You know you can trust me, right?' She winced slightly at the words she had used. She knew she was touching one of Astrid's sore spots. Her sister didn't like Freya to think she didn't trust her.

'Of course you'll be fine,' Astrid said, and now it was if their roles were reversed and Astrid was trying to convince Freya that everything would be okay.

'Exactly. It's one little childhood illness,' Freya said, thinking it couldn't possibly be that bad since millions of parents managed to survive the experience each year.

'I'll call again tonight.'

'The kids would love to talk to you.'

'I have to go.' It was clear from Astrid's tone that she wanted to do anything but hang up the phone.

'I know. Now go do your civic duty thing,' Freya said with a laugh.

After her sister ended the call, she

leant her head back on the sofa and wondered if she could squeeze in a short nap herself, since Daisy was sleeping too.

Her ringing phone woke her, and when she looked at the screen she realised it was Benji's school. She almost laughed, since she had a pretty good idea what they were ringing to tell her.

17

'Miss Hardy, this is Mrs Jones, the school administrator. I'm afraid young Benji's not very well.'

'Don't tell me — he has a rash and you think its chickenpox.'

There was a pause at the other end of the line. 'How did you know?' Mrs Jones asked, as if she expected Freya to tell her she'd received some sort of telepathic message.

'Let's just say he's not the only spotty child in this household.'

'Oh dear,' Mrs Jones said, sounding like she meant it. 'Does that mean poor Daisy has it too?'

'I'm afraid so. The good news is that Lily has already had it, so her mother tells me she can't get it again.'

'Well that's true, dear, thankfully. I suspect we're going to have another mini-outbreak here too. I appreciate that Daisy isn't well, but would you be able to come and pick Benji up? We'd like to try and keep his contact with the other children to a minimum if possible.'

'Of course,' Freya said, standing up and shifting Daisy in her arms. 'We'll be there shortly.'

'Is there anything you need? Calamine is very good for the itching. I could pick you some up and drop it by.'

'That's very sweet of you, Mrs Jones, but Astrid keeps a well-stocked medicine cabinet. I think we'll be just fine.'

⋆ ⋆ ⋆

Daisy slept the whole way up the hill to the school. Mrs Jones was waiting with Benji in the school office. Freya took one look at him and stopped in her tracks.

'Oh wow, Benji, that's a lot of spots!'

The little boy grinned. Clearly he was feeling okay despite his spotty appearance. It seemed to Freya that there was no part of him that was spot-free. He was literally covered from head to foot.

'That happened fast,' she said, almost as a question, since she knew next to nothing about chickenpox.

'I know,' Benji said, lifting up his school T-shirt. 'I only had one last night, and now look at me. I've lost count!'

Freya stared at him. 'Why didn't you say anything?'

He shrugged. 'I forgot.'

'I'm really sorry, Mrs Jones,' Freya said, realising the implication of Benji's words. Had she known before that morning, she could have kept Benji at home and away from the other children.

'Don't be silly, dear. Benji himself probably caught it from one of the other children here. It's just one of those things. Now let me give you my number at home. Please ring me if you need anything, anything at all.'

She handed over a piece of paper, which Freya took with a grateful smile.

It was nice to know there was someone close by she could call on if things got desperate, someone other than the confusing Mr Barnes. Since it was difficult to predict whether he would respond or if it would be Jamie, it felt safer and less bewildering to avoid him.

★　★　★

When Lily got home, both Benji and Daisy were covered in spots, which in turn were covered in pale pink lotion. Daisy was wearing mittens and Benji was trying not to scratch, since Freya had only five minutes before threatened him with his own set of mittens. She felt like she had things under control and was feeling rather pleased with herself.

'What have you done to them?' Lily asked in such an incredulous way that Freya felt the need to come to her own defence.

'I haven't done anything,' she said indignantly.

'We've got chickenpox,' Benji said with a certain amount of glee. 'And I've got more spots than Daisy.' He said it as if he had just broken the world one-hundred-metre-sprint record.

Lily lifted a hand, covered in the arm of her jumper, across her mouth and glared at Freya, who once again got the impression that things were entirely her fault.

'Relax,' Freya told her. 'You can't get it. Your mum said you've already had it.'

'Are you sure?' Lily's voice was muffled by her jumper and her hand.

'When is your mum ever not sure about stuff like that?'

Lily shrugged as if to concede that point. 'But I think I should go stay at Steph's.'

For once Freya wondered if she was right. It wasn't like she was going to be able to give Lily much of her attention. 'I'll ring your mum in a bit and ask her,' she said.

Lily bounced on the balls of her feet, which Freya took to be a sign that she was pleased, and then watched her niece run out of the room. 'Got homework to do!' she shouted, which Freya was pretty sure was pre-teen speak for 'I need to be anywhere but here.'

'Stop scratching!' Benji said, which pulled Freya's attention back to the room.

'I'm not,' Daisy insisted, while clearly running her mittened hands up and down her legs.

'Are too,' Benji said, and at that point Daisy swatted him and managed, judging by the yowling, to catch his eye. She took a deep breath and then stepped in to separate them and soothe them in equal measures.

At half past eight, both the spotty ones were in bed and finally asleep. And after a conversation with Astrid, Lily was now happily staying at her friend's house. Astrid had agreed to a couple of days to begin with, and Freya had to agree that it was probably the best thing for all of them right now.

She had the freezer door open and was staring inside to look for something to eat. It wasn't that the freezer wasn't full; it was more that it was full of healthy home-cooked food, and what Freya really fancied was chips or an Indian or maybe pizza. She sighed and closed the door, wondering if Astrid had any takeaway menus secretly hidden away. She thought it was unlikely, since Astrid was staunchly against any kind of junk food.

The doorbell chimed and Freya rushed to answer it, hoping that the children would not be disturbed. The only thing she could think was that Lily had changed her mind or had a fight with Steph and wanted to come home. But when she opened the door, she was surprised to see Mr Barnes. He was carrying a brown paper bag which, judging from the smell, contained some sort of Indian food. For a moment Freya just stopped and stared. Being around this man was beginning to feel like she had whiplash from trying to keep up with his changing personality. Here he was with food, and she wondered if this time he intended to actually stay and eat it.

'Hello,' she said uncertainly, not really sure what else to say.

Jamie — for it seemed certain it was Jamie who was standing on her doorstep — smiled. 'I figured that with two sick kids, you wouldn't have had time to eat, so I thought I'd bring you some food.'

'Thanks,' Freya said, still not certain what was going on.

'Can I come in?' he asked with an amused smile, as if it was Freya who was being weird and not his previous abrupt exit that was causing the problem.

'I don't know, can you?' Freya didn't try to keep the sarcasm from her voice.

Jamie's face looked confused for a moment and then resolved into understanding. 'Ah, I suppose you're referring to last time.'

She nodded and raised an eyebrow.

'Yes . . . you know, when you practically ran out of here without even finishing your drink?'

'I was a little concerned about professional boundaries,' he said, and Freya just stared. When he didn't say anything else, she knew she would have to speak, or they would spend the whole evening standing on the door-step.

'And now you're not?'

'I've had time to think about it, and I think we can manage.'

'Manage what exactly?' Freya felt like there was a story behind all this bizarre behaviour, but she couldn't figure it out from the few cues that he was giving her. He looked down at his feet, seemingly annoyed. She wasn't sure if it was because she wasn't getting what-ever it was he was trying to say, or because he was hoping they could just move on from this obviously frustrating conversation.

'Let's just say that I've had a bad experience of crossing boundaries, and

I don't want to make the same mistake again, for everyone's sake.'

Freya blinked. Jamie looked almost stricken at the memory. 'Okay, I get it. Sort of. Come in.'

18

Freya could have pushed him for more information — she had to admit she was curious — but that didn't seem the right thing to do just now. Jamie made his way to the kitchen and started unpacking the plastic containers.

'I got a bit of everything. I wasn't sure what you liked.'

Freya grabbed a couple of plates from the cupboard. 'When it comes to Indian, I pretty much like everything, especially after the day I've had.'

He pulled the beer caps off and handed her a bottle. 'I hope beer's okay?' he asked, looking at her for the first time since he had walked in.

'It's fine,' she said taking a seat.

There was silence as they each dished themselves up some food. Freya had to admit it smelt great, and also that the company of someone other than poorly children was a bonus.

'Kids asleep?' Jamie asked, which Freya felt was pretty obvious, but it was probably a good safe conversation to start with.

'Yep. Both of the poorly ones are wearing mittens to stop them from scratching, and are covered in calamine. Lily's at Steph's. Not sure how long the kids will sleep, though; they're pretty uncomfortable.' She took a mouthful of rice and curry. 'You've had chickenpox, right?' She looked up at him and he laughed out loud. The noise startled her a little, but she had to admit she liked it when he laughed.

'I've been a teacher for ten years. I've literally had every childhood illness there is. Most teachers spend their first few years being sick.'

Freya nodded. 'Must be one of the down sides.'

He shrugged. 'Yeah, but I love it. I mean, don't get me wrong — it can be stressful and all that. But I wouldn't want to do anything else.'

Freya took a moment to digest that information. 'I'm kind of envious,' she said.

Jamie took a swig of beer and his face registered a question.

'I studied History of Art at uni. It's kind of my thing I guess, but not so easy to find employment in, if you know what I mean.' He nodded, and she took that as a sign to keep talking. 'I've had a couple of jobs at commercial art galleries, but it's not really what I want to do; and to be honest the pay is pretty awful, which makes surviving in London difficult.'

'Do you paint?' Jamie asked, and she felt like she had his full attention. It was always nice when someone was prepared to listen to her.

'No,' she said with a smile. 'I wish I could, but I have absolutely no talent in that area. But that doesn't mean I don't love art, and what I enjoy most is sharing it with others.'

'So your ideal job would be . . . ?'

'In a public gallery somewhere. But

the jobs are few and far between, and so I've decided to take some time out.' Jamie nodded as if he understood. 'My plan was to visit with Astrid and the kids and then go travelling. I think some distance might help me figure out what I want from my life; what might make me happy in the long term.'

Jamie took his last mouthful and leaned back in his chair. 'I never really got the travelling bug. I always wanted to find somewhere to call home.'

'And have you found it?' Freya asked curiously. She couldn't really imagine settling in the small village at this point in her life, even though she loved Astrid and the rest of the family.

'Not sure,' he said, and his face was a little wistful. 'I thought I'd found it before, so I want to take my time here before I make any big decisions.'

Freya pondered this and wondered if it was time to ask the burning question: what happened the time before, and did it have anything to do with the professional boundaries comment from earlier?

'Where did you grow up?' she asked instead, figuring that it was a safe question and might lead him to open up.

'Here and there.' Catching her expression, he added, 'My dad was in the army, so we were never anywhere for long. I think that's why I'm keen to find 'home'. We travelled and lived all over. We didn't stay anywhere for more than a couple of years.'

'That must've been tough.' Freya said, thinking of her own childhood in which she had lived in one place until she had left home for university.

He shrugged. 'Army brats are used to it. You make friends with other army kids quickly, but a part of you knows it won't last, so it's not the same as it is for other kids, I guess. What about you?'

'We lived in the same place all my life. We never really went anywhere; my mum was pretty sick for most of my childhood. Astrid is ten years older, so she was basically like a mum to me.'

'And your mum?'

'She died when I was sixteen.'

'I'm sorry.'

Now it was Freya's turn to shrug. 'Don't get me wrong; it was a really tough time. But it had always been a possibility all my life, and I was lucky that I had Astrid and then Mike.'

Jamie seemed thoughtful. 'But Astrid and the kids don't move around with Mike?'

Freya shook her head. 'No. They both decided that they wanted the children to have some stability, and Mike's job in the army is one that means he can be sent anywhere at any time, so it's not really a case that they would see more of him if they were to live on base.'

'From personal experience I would say that was a wise choice.'

Freya smiled. 'One of the reasons they could make that choice was because they inherited some money after our mum died. I guess not everyone is that fortunate.'

'I guess,' Jamie said, but he didn't sound exactly convinced.

'Shall we go sit in the lounge? It's a bit more comfortable than these kitchen chairs. Unless you need to go?'

He made a show of glancing at his watch. 'Maybe a quick coffee first. It's a school night and I have to get up in the morning, even if you don't.'

Freya walked into the kitchen, followed by Jamie, and flicked the switch on the kettle. 'Seriously?' she said in reply to his comment. 'You think chickenpox will mean a lie-in? More like the opposite! You know a lot about teaching kids, but not so much about raising them.' Freya said it lightly with a smile as a bit of a tease, but Jamie's face registered a completely different reaction. He looked first shocked and then as if she had slapped him.

She reached out a hand for his arm. 'I'm sorry; that was a joke. I didn't mean it as some kind of backward insult.'

Jamie took a step back from her. He

looked as if he was trying hard to get his emotions in check. 'It's okay,' he said after a few moments had passed. 'Just ancient history that doesn't always feel so ancient.'

Freya nodded as if she understood; but really it was just another tiny piece of the puzzle that was Jamie/Mr Barnes, and at present she had no idea what the overall picture would look like. 'Again, I'm sorry. I never intended . . . '

Jamie held up a hand. 'Forget it.' And Freya saw him smile with some effort. 'It's the past, and I shouldn't have brought it up. How about I help you with the coffee?' He picked up the tray with the two mugs and sugar bowl and walked away from her, heading to the lounge.

Freya watched him go, wondering if she would ever figure out the mystery that was Jamie Barnes, or if he would ever let her.

19

The last six days had been a blur of unhappy, itchy children, and Freya was exhausted. Jamie popped in every few evenings, and Jan brought the odd dinner, but other than that Freya was left alone in a house seemingly full of sick children. Daisy and Benji slept when they felt like it, so that inevitably meant that they were awake at odd hours during the night, when they seemed to have a surprising amount of energy. All Freya could really think about was getting through the next hour and trying to keep her somewhat frayed temper.

'Benji, please don't do that,' she said, trying to speak and take a calming deep breath at the same time. 'You know it winds Daisy up.'

'But I had it first,' Benji said, pouting like his little sister.

'Yes, but in this family we share,' Freya said, using an expression that now just tripped off her tongue like she was a professional parent.

Benji threw the plastic ball in the direction of his sister and it bounced off the coffee table, knocking over two glasses of milk. He froze, and even Daisy stopped yelling long enough to look slightly concerned. 'Sorry, Auntie Freya,' he said.

Freya stood up and opened the glass patio door. 'Why don't you take the ball outside and play with Daisy?' She tried to keep her voice light-hearted. After all, Benji hadn't knocked over the glasses on purpose, and she knew that she was feeling as stir-crazy as the kids were.

'I help you clean up,' Daisy said as she used a toy dustpan and brush to spread the milk so that it ran off the side of the coffee table and started to dribble on the floor. Freya clenched her jaw and tried to think of her happy place.

'Let's go play, Daisy,' Benji said, hurriedly risking a quick glance at his aunt's face. 'I think Auntie Freya can manage without our help.' He grabbed his sister by the hand and pulled her into the back garden.

Freya made her way to the kitchen to find the carpet cleaner, which she hoped would do the trick on the spreading milk stain. On her third attempt she managed to open the child lock on the under-sink cupboard and pulled out the bottle. But she didn't have to shake it to know that it was empty; she had been doing a lot of carpet cleaning since the kids had been sick and had forgotten to ask Jamie or Jan to get her some more. She could hear the happy squeals of the children in the garden and so decided that she had five minutes to feel sorry for herself. She sat down on the floor, leaned her head against the kitchen cupboard, and closed her eyes.

The next thing she knew, a hand was

shaking her and calling her name. 'Freya?'

'Just five more minutes, kids,' she said croakily as she tried to work out why she was so uncomfortable.

'Freya, it's Jamie. Are you all right?'

Her eyes flashed open as she tried to remember the last thing that had happened. She rubbed a hand across her face and frowned as she realised that she was slumped on the floor in the kitchen, and she tried to work out what she had forgotten. Then fear sliced through her. 'Benji, Daisy?' she yelled, trying to get to her feet and search for the children at the same time. She managed to stand but her head swam, and she felt herself stumble as two arms reached out to steady her.

'Relax, Freya. They're fine. They were in the garden when I called round. I did ring the doorbell, but when I got no answer, Benji let me in round the back.'

'I must've fallen asleep,' Freya mumbled as she took a step away from

Jamie and tried to process all the information. 'I was looking for carpet cleaner . . . ' Her voice trailed off as she saw the empty bottle on the floor beside where she had been sitting. When she looked at Jamie, he had such an expression of concern that she wasn't sure whether she should be cross or dissolve into his arms in tears. The burning behind her eyes told her that the latter was more likely.

'I need to clean the carpet. We spilt milk. It's going to smell so bad.' The words came jumbled out of her mouth, and Freya knew she wasn't making much sense.

'What you need is to go to bed,' Jamie said, taking hold of her arm and steering her towards the kitchen door.

'I have to watch the children,' she said somewhat crossly. Of course she needed to sleep — all parents needed sleep, for crying out loud. But that was a luxury they weren't afforded.

'I'm going to watch the kids,' Jamie said. 'In fact, I'll take them up the park to run off some steam and then get them something to eat. That should give you a couple of hours to catch up on some shuteye.'

'They're infectious,' Freya said, slurring her words slightly as if she was drunk.

'Freya, half the village has chickenpox, and the other half has either already been in contact or had it before, so I think we'll be fine.'

'You're sure you don't mind?' She forced herself to say it, even though she knew she would probably cry if he changed his mind. Her bed was definitely calling to her.

'I don't mind,' he said softly. Since she was swaying on the spot trying to make her legs obey her, he gently took hold of one of her hands and guided her up the stairs. Once in her room, he pulled back the duvet, and Freya was asleep almost before her head hit the pillow.

'Get some sleep,' someone said, and she was pretty sure it was Jamie.

When Freya woke, her bedroom was filled with morning sun. One glance at her phone told her she'd slept right through from four o'clock the previous afternoon until now, six in the morning. She rolled out of bed and found her slippers. A quick peek in the kids' rooms told her that they were still fast asleep. She crept downstairs, all her thoughts focused on making coffee and drinking it in the peace and quiet.

With hot coffee in one hand and a chocolate biscuit in the other, she padded into the lounge. Her first reaction was to scream, but she managed to bite it back down; she didn't want to scare the children, and she certainly didn't want to see what was on the floor in the lounge: a long lumpy shape in what looked like a black bin liner. Someone had been murdered in their house while they slept!

Freya crept over to where the house phone sat in its cradle and as quietly as possible picked it up, all the while her eyes darting around the room checking for any sign of the other intruder. She pressed the first nine and winced as the phone made a loud beeping noise; clearly Daisy had been playing with it again.

At that moment the shape moved, and this time Freya didn't hold back a scream.

'Freya! What the hell's the matter?' Jamie said as he struggled to fight his way out of his sleeping bag and find his feet.

Freya felt all the breath in her lungs rush out, and she blindly sought out an armchair and sat down. 'You scared me!' she said.

'I scared you?' he echoed angrily, although whether it was fear or embarrassment talking, Freya wasn't sure. She watched as he continued to try to escape the confines of his sleeping bag.

'I thought you were . . . ' Her voice trailed off as she looked away and tried to work out how to explain that she thought some stranger had broken into the house and left behind a dead body, which seemed beyond ridiculous to her now. Then she caught sight of Jamie's face, which seemed transfixed in horror, and Freya couldn't help but risk a glance over her shoulder. 'What?' she said when with relief she realised that they were quite alone.

'I think we have a bigger problem.' Jamie lifted a hand to point right at her.

20

'Very funny,' Freya said grumpily as she tried to smooth down her bed hair. She could feel the colour rise in her cheeks. 'I've been looking after sick kids for a week; of course I look a state. So kind of you to point out,' she added, feeling a little guilty at having a go at the man who had allowed her a full fourteen hours of sleep.

She forced herself to look back up at him. 'Sorry. Always a bit grumpy before I've had my first coffee.' She tried a smile, but Jamie continued to look slightly horrified. 'Okay, the joke's over. Enough already.'

He walked over to her and held out his hand. Freya frowned at it, but with a roll of her eyes took it and allowed herself to be led out into the hallway. 'What?' she said, wondering if Jamie had lost the plot and perhaps was much stranger than she had at first thought.

'Look,' he said, before gently turning her face towards the long mirror that hung in the hallway.

Freya took a step back when she caught a glimpse of herself, and all at once knew why Jamie had been so horrified. She was covered in spots — not acne spots, but oozy, raw chickenpox spots. 'Oh, you have got to be kidding me,' she said to her reflection before catching the amused look in Jamie's eyes.

'I take it you never had chickenpox as a child?' He sounded as incredulous as Freya felt.

'Not according to Astrid, and she would know. Or maybe it's shingles?'

'Nope, you can't get shingles from chickenpox, only the other way round.'

Freya stepped up close to the mirror so she could see her vast array of spots more closely. 'Well I guess this explains why I was so tired yesterday.' Suddenly feeling as if she had a million ants crawling over her skin, she reached across her belly and surreptitiously gave it a quick scratch.

'Enough of that,' Jamie said in his best teacher voice before he grabbed her hand.

'But it itches,' she whined, unable to keep a straight face.

'Well at least I stocked you up with calamine.'

She took one last look at herself in the mirror and sighed, fighting the urge to scratch her back against the doorpost as Daisy had done.

'Yep, but I don't think the mittens will fit,' Jamie said with a laugh. And then a thundering of footsteps told them that the children were awake. Benji was wide-eyed with horror.

'Auntie Freya, your face!' he said loudly, pointing at her.

Jamie was working hard not to laugh, and Freya gave him the 'look'.

'Did we share our chickenpox with you?' the boy asked, turning his head to one side and looking at his aunt as if she was an interesting specimen on his science programme.

'I think you did, kiddo.'

'Mummy says sharing is good,' Daisy piped up, and then they all laughed.

'Daisy has a point,' Jamie said once he had stopped laughing, just in time for him and Benji to start giggling again. 'Look, I'll get them breakfast. Why don't you go and do the bath and calamine thing.'

Freya studied Jamie's face, but could only see a willingness to help out. 'Don't you have other things you should be doing?' she asked, and winced at the tone she had used. 'What I meant was — '

Jamie held up his hand, and to Freya's relief he smiled. 'I know exactly what you meant. I had nothing planned this weekend but marking, and when you're up to taking over for a bit I can pop home and get it. I can mark and keep an eye on the kids, so you can rest up.' And with that he turned his back on her and herded the kids into the kitchen.

Freya watched him go. That familiar confusion she felt around him was back. One minute he wouldn't stay for a beer, and the next he was offering to co-parent. She walked up the stairs and tried to work out how she felt about it. But as she turned on the taps and dumped rock salt into the bath, as she had been doing for the kids all week, all she could feel was relieved that she had some help. And who knew — maybe that was all it was. But Freya couldn't ignore the nagging feeling that something had changed between them. She just wasn't sure what that something was.

★ ★ ★

Later that evening, while Freya was reading Benji a bedtime story, she could hear movement in the kitchen, and the occasional clatter of a pan, and it wasn't long before delicious smells started to waft up the stairs. She bent over and kissed her nephew, whose eyes were drooping with sleep, and quietly made her way downstairs.

Despite the noises, the kitchen was very tidy and organised. Jamie seemed to approach cooking as if it were a military exercise. He turned when he heard her enter the room, and she tried to hide her grin at the sight of him in Astrid's frilly flowery apron. Admittedly he had folded it in half and only wore the bottom half, but it seemed such a contrast to Jamie's well-built body and black T-shirt that she couldn't help but giggle.

'It was the only one I could find,' he said with a shrug and a grin. Clearly that sort of thing did not worry him one bit, and for Freya that was another tick on the positive list. She shook her head — not that she had any sort of list where Jamie Barnes was concerned, of course.

'Something wrong?' he asked. Obviously he had noticed her shaking her head.

'No,' she said, turning away to busy

herself laying cutlery on the table to give her face a chance to return to its usual colour. 'Just impressed you can cook.'

'Dad taught me,' he said, reaching for the cupboard where Astrid kept all her spices, 'when he was home.'

'It's tough having parents away, that's for sure.'

'I can still remember what it felt like, particularly at Lily's age. It was hard not to resent my dad for not being around when I needed him.'

'Thankfully Lily and her dad are really close.'

Jamie nodded, lost in thought. 'But he won't be able to rely on that forever. Lily is getting to the age where they question everything. Blind devotion won't be the factor it was when she was younger.'

Freya reached into a cupboard for wine glasses. That was not a nice thought, but although she resented him for saying it out loud, she knew that it was something that both Astrid and

Mike worried about. She put the glasses on the table. 'Are we having red or white?' she asked, gesturing to the two bottles that Jamie had brought with the rest of the supplies.

'Wasn't sure what you preferred. I'm making lamb shanks, so red is best if you like it.'

'Sounds perfect,' Freya said, unscrewing the cap so that it could 'breathe'. She had no idea what that meant, but she had been told enough times by a previous boyfriend that it was an automatic response. 'What do you think Mike should do?' she asked, taking a seat at the table since she couldn't think of any other jobs to do to help out.

'Quit the army,' Jamie said with his back to her.

Freya let out a bark of laughter. Like that was going to happen. 'I'm not sure that's an option,' she said.

Jamie was still for a moment, then turned to look at her, and she could see from his face that it hadn't been a flippant suggestion. Her face blanched as she realised he was being serious. 'Sorry,' she said. 'I thought you were joking.'

'My dad was away for most of my teenage years, and by the time he retired from the army we were basically strangers. We're working on being father and son now, but we've lost a lot of years.'

Freya could see the pain of that clearly written on his face, where she could also see the echo of his teenage self. She stood up, and before she could change her mind she walked over to him and placed a hand on his arm.

'That must be really tough.' She watched as he seemed to try and swallow down the emotion.

'It is, but we're lucky that we have this second chance. You must miss your mum,' he added, and Freya knew he was changing the subject, but that he needed to do so.

'I do in many ways, but she was never really able to be a mum to me, or at least not in the way the child-me wanted. Don't get me wrong; I know that it was never her fault. She always did whatever she was well enough to do. But more often than not, Astrid would step into the breach.'

She moved to sit on the counter-top. 'I miss the little things, I guess. She always, always would do my hair in the morning before school. If she couldn't get out of bed, I'd climb up beside her, and she'd do the most elaborate plaits. She always loved my hair,' she said instinctively, reaching for her long locks as if to check they were still there. 'I've never cut it short. It'd seem disloyal.' She blinked, realising tears were building at the corners of her eyes. 'Sorry,' she mumbled, brushing them away.

'No need,' Jamie said simply, moving to her side and using his thumb to brush away a stray tear. They stared at each other for a couple of heartbeats. Their experiences were so different, but in so many ways similar, and understanding made Freya want to reach for Jamie as he had reached for her on the night that Lily had gone missing. But she didn't have a chance, as she felt Jamie's arms wrap around her and hold her close.

She was certain she could have stayed like that forever, but a hiss and a splashing noise told them both that things were happening on the hob.

'Oops,' Jamie said, disentangling himself from Freya's arms with a look of reluctance that made her heart skip. 'First rule of cooking — no distractions.' He turned to grin at her, and Freya was sure that she was a happy distraction rather than anything else.

21

Freya pushed her plate away. She didn't think she'd ever eaten anything quite so delicious. 'Are you sure you're not a chef on the side?' she said.

Jamie laughed. It was a sound she'd come to love, and she loved it even more when she was the cause. 'Nah,' he said. 'I love to cook, but teaching children how to do it is so much more fun.'

'You're lucky that you've found the thing you love and you can earn a living from it,' Freya said ruefully, thinking about the awful jobs she'd had since graduation, and her decision to go and travel the world.

Jamie was looking at her thoughtfully. 'Do you think you're going to find what you're looking for out there?' he asked, waving a hand in the general direction of 'the world'.

She shrugged. 'Don't know really, but it's not just about that. I've spent most of my adult life listening to Mike's stories of far-flung places, and I guess I want to go and see them for myself.' Jamie nodded as if he understood, but Freya wasn't sure he quite got it.

'And what if you found what you were looking for here?' he asked, his voice soft and husky as if he was afraid to speak the words out loud.

Freya flinched a little. She knew deep down that the conversation had been moving in this direction, but she was surprised that he had come right out and said it. 'Believe me, Astrid's been keeping any eye out in the couple of local public galleries, but jobs are like hen's teeth.' She tried to add levity to her voice to test the meaning of his words. When he leaned towards her, she found she was hypnotised by his gaze and couldn't look away.

'That's not quite what I meant, you know.'

She whispered, 'I know,' and then his lips found hers and they kissed.

The rat-a-tat-tat on the window made them both jump, and they broke apart like guilty teenagers. They stared at each other, wondering if they had somehow both imagined it — and then there it was again.

Freya reached behind her for the cord to the venetian blinds and pulled them up halfway. With the kitchen light on, it was hard to see who was outside banging on the window so late in the evening. Then a face appeared pressed against the glass, and Freya knew exactly who it was. In one movement she pushed Jamie away and slid down off the counter-top.

'It's Lily,' she hissed as if her niece would be able to hear her outside.

'I know,' Jamie hissed back. 'I can see that. Why are we whispering?'

'She just saw us kiss!' Freya said in an exasperated squeak.

'I'm pretty sure we aren't the first people she's seen kissing,' he said, and now he looked amused, which some-how made Freya feel more foolish.

'She has this thing that we're all 'lovey-dovey' about each other,' Freya said by way of explanation.

'Well, I'm pretty sure she's right,' Jamie said, and then leaned in to kiss her again.

For a moment Freya forgot that her niece was outside, forgot that she was probably watching them right now, and lost herself in the embrace.

The next knock on the glass was the sort that a parent might make, sharp and annoyed. Freya opened one eye and could just about make out that Lily was standing there with her arms folded and an eyebrow raised. She forced herself to focus and took a step back from Jamie. 'I should probably let her in and find out why she's here,' she said with a frown. She moved away and Jamie reached out for her hand.

'Probably a good idea — but remember, you're the parent.' There was a twinkle in his eye, and Freya wasn't sure if he meant that Lily had apparently walked home in the dark (a real no-no), or that she seemed to disapprove of them kissing.

'Lily, honey, is everything all right?' Freya asked as she opened the door and used one hand to surreptitiously smooth down her hair that Jamie had been running his hands through. She narrowed her eyes. 'Did you walk here by yourself?'

'No,' Lily said as if Freya had asked the most obvious question in the world. 'I told Jan that I wanted to come home tonight, and she asked Jason to walk me back.'

'Who's Jason?' Freya asked.

'Steph's older brother,' Lily said in a tone that suggested Freya should know.

'How much older?' Freya asked suspiciously, and then instantly knew she had said the wrong thing, judging by the look of pure disdain on Lily's face.

'You're one to talk,' Lily snapped, and Freya was pretty sure it was not an acceptable response from a pre-teen to their parental figure. She tried to frame a response, but Lily just tutted in irritation and pushed past her.

Freya reached out and gently took her hand. 'Hang on a minute, Lil. You haven't told me why you've come home. Is everything all right?'

Lily glared at her. 'I spoke to Mum, and she said you weren't well and that you would need help with the kids.' She looked away from her aunt to stare scathingly at Jamie, who was standing in the doorway. He had obviously heard everything and had decided to stay silent. 'But it looks like not only do you not need my help, but you wanted me out of the way.' And with that, she stormed upstairs and slammed the door to her bedroom.

Freya sighed and absent-mindedly scratched at a spot on her neck. A hand reached out and gently pulled her fingers away.

'Stop scratching; it'll scar,' Jamie said softly.

'Why do I get the feeling I've just experienced yet another epic parenting fail?'

Jamie tugged her back into the kitchen and gently closed the door. 'Whatever that seemed to be about, it was really about the fact that we were kissing.'

'It seemed like it to me,' Freya said gloomily, and she let herself be pulled in to a hug.

'Lily's lashing out at you because you're the nearest person. I suspect she's upset about her mum and dad, or maybe she's had a fight with Steph.'

'So why is she yelling at me and making me feel guilty for spending time with you?'

Jamie shrugged and planted a kiss on a spot-free place on Freya's forehead. 'Because she's nearly a teenager and her emotions are all over the place. And you're a safe person to lash out at.' Freya made a quizzical face. 'She knows that you'll still be here in the morning when she might

197

be ready to talk,' he said.

She nodded in understanding. How was it that Jamie, who was not a parent and had certainly never been an eleven-year-old-girl, understood this better than she did?

'I deal with a lot of emotional eleven-year-olds at school,' he said, as if he could read her mind. 'I'm going to go. I don't think my presence here is helping.'

Freya reached for him. 'It's helping me,' she murmured.

'I didn't say I *wanted* to go, but I think you need to get some sleep and then talk to Lily in the morning. If you need anything, text me, and I'll be right over.' He kissed her one last time. 'And let me know as soon as it's safe, and I'll be back.'

He grinned at her and then left her standing in the kitchen alone, thinking about that last kiss.

22

Freya rolled over in bed and stared, bleary-eyed, at the illuminated alarm clock. It was twenty past nine. She lay her head back on the pillow and wondered when the last time was that she had slept so late. As she smiled at the thought, there was something else nagging at her, but her sleepy brain couldn't put its proverbial finger on it.

Her eyes opened wide as she remembered the children, who had probably been unsupervised for over three hours, and she leapt out of bed. Her feet found the floor, but it felt as if it was titling badly, and she couldn't find her balance. She reached out both arms to try and stabilise herself, and the next thing she knew she had crumpled down with a thud.

There was the sound of thundering feet on the stairs, and then her bedroom door was thrown open. 'Are you okay?' Lily said as she knelt down beside her aunt. 'Should I call a doctor or an ambulance or Mr Barnes?'

Freya knew that she had to have frightened Lily if she was prepared to call Jamie. She shook her head. 'None of the above, Lil. I'm fine; just stood up too quickly.'

Lily still looked concerned, but put an arm under Freya's and heaved them both to their feet. Freya wobbled a bit and so Lily guided her back to bed.

'You don't look fine,' her niece said in a tone that could only have come from Astrid. 'You look like you need to be in bed. Stay there and I'll bring you up a coffee and some breakfast.'

Freya laughed, although she had to admit the idea of staying in bed was a nice one. 'I can't stay in bed, hon. I have to look after Daisy and Benji.'

Lily pulled a pillow from the wardrobe and indicated that her aunt should sit forward. Not knowing what else to do, Freya obeyed. 'I can look after the kids,' Lily said. 'I've been up with them since six, and no one's burned the house down or put any beads up their nose.'

She pursed her lips as if she was trying not to smile and Freya laughed, knowing that her niece was desperate to giggle. Once they had stopped, Freya knew she needed to get serious. 'That wasn't our agreement, Lil. It's not your job to look after the kids. You're only eleven.'

Lily snorted as she picked up some of Freya's discarded clothes and pushed them into the full laundry bin. 'Who do you think looks after them when Mum's ill?'

'Your mum's never ill,' Freya said; and then watching Lily's expression change, she added, 'Why didn't she call me to come and help out?'

'Because she didn't need to — she had me,' Lily said with exaggerated slowness, as if Freya was having trouble understanding. She walked towards the door, dragging the laundry bin behind her. 'If it'll make you feel better, I could call Mr Barnes.' She turned back to Freya, her expression watchful, and Freya took that as a sign that she was ready to talk about last night.

'I could,' Freya said thoughtfully, 'but not if it makes you uncomfortable, Lil.'

Her niece left the laundry bin by the door and crossed the room to the bed. Freya shifted a little and Lily sat on the edge. She reached out a hand for Lily's, and for once she wasn't rejected.

'Do you like him — I mean, like that?' Lily asked.

Freya smiled. 'I think so, but we only really just met, Lily. It's nothing serious, I promise.'

The girl nodded, and it seemed like she was having trouble finding the words she wanted to say. Freya wasn't sure whether she was going to get yelled at or if Lily was going to cry.

'You're not going to leave us, then,' Lily mumbled, looking at their inter-linked hands.

If it hadn't been such a serious

moment, Freya felt sure she would have laughed at the ridiculousness of that idea. Instead she squeezed Lily's hand. 'Is that what you're worried about?'

Lily's head remained lowered, so Freya brushed the curtain of hair out of the way so she could see her face, which was displaying a whole mixture of emotions but mainly revealed a scared little girl. 'Lily, I need you to understand something. I am not going to leave you. Not for Mr Barnes, not for any possible reason until your mum is back here with you. I promise.'

Lily nodded, and Freya felt a tear drop onto her hands.

'Oh Lil. Why didn't you tell me?'

Suddenly Freya had her hands full as Lily threw herself into her arms. She held her niece and rocked her, and eventually Lily sat up. Her face was tear-stained, but she was wearing a small smile. 'I'm silly,' she said, looking embarrassed.

'No,' Freya said firmly, 'you're not silly; but you could save yourself a whole lot of grief if you just spoke to me about some of this stuff.' They grinned at each other.

'I'd better go and check on the kids,' Lily said, standing up. 'I left them watching a DVD and it's probably about to finish.'

'I'll just have a shower and I'll be down.'

'No you won't,' said Lily, again channelling her mum. 'You'll stay in bed until at least lunchtime — and,' she said with one hand on the door, 'if you don't feel like getting up this afternoon, I'll call Mr Barnes.' She had a mischievous glint in her eye, and Freya felt like she had her niece back.

* * *

Freya wasn't sure how long she had been asleep; it could have been a couple of minutes or several hours. She lay still, listening for the sounds of the children downstairs; but as hard as she strained her ears, she couldn't hear anything at all. She felt her heart speed up. Although new to the parenting thing, she had been around long enough to know that silence wasn't golden; it spelt trouble.

Fighting the temptation to leap out of bed, she slid her feet to the floor and allowed her brain a few moments to acclimatise to being upright. Ignoring the urgent itching messages that seemed to be coming from every part of her body, she made her way to the door and pulled it open.

Still nothing. Even if the children were watching TV, she should be able to hear the low drone from the landing. She made her way downstairs.

'Lily? Benji?' She added in desperation, 'Daisy?'

Her heart was beating faster now, and she was having trouble controlling the rising panic. She remembered her last conversation with Lily quite clearly. Her niece had seemed okay; there were certainly no signs that she was preparing to run away again. Or were there?

Freya found herself pulling open cupboard doors in the kitchen, looking for the children. She knew she was being ridiculous, since not even Daisy could fit, but they had to be somewhere. She ran from room to room, but there was no sign of them. Freya's mind went into overdrive, but one thought kept rising to the surface: the children had been kidnapped. Her heart lurched one more time and she reached for the phone.

23

Her fingers fumbled to press the 9 three times. The call was answered and she was greeted with: 'Emergency services. What service do you require?'

She heard a key turn in the lock to the front door. With the phone held to her ear, she ran into the hall. 'Where have you been?' she yelled at Lily, who was first through the door.

'Ma'am, can you tell me what the emergency is?'

Freya found herself looking around for the source of the voice and then realised it was coming from the phone, which she still held up to her ear. 'I'm very sorry,' she said, blushing, although for whose benefit she wasn't sure. 'I thought my nieces were missing but I've just found them. I'm sorry to waste your time.'

'No problem, ma'am. Please call us

back if you need to.'

Freya wondered if the efficient voice at the end of the line believed her, but forced her attention onto all three of the children, who were now standing in the doorway looking somewhat confused. 'Where have you been?' she yelled again. 'What were you thinking, going out on your own? I've just called the police!' Freya knew that she was getting hysterical but couldn't seem to calm down.

Lily raised an eyebrow. 'We *weren't* on our own,' she said as if that were the most ridiculous thing anyone had ever suggested.

The door was pushed back, and legs and the biggest teddy bear that Freya had ever seen stepped into the hall. 'They were with me, of course. Didn't you read our note?' The voice was somewhat muffled by fur, but Freya knew instantly who it was. She had made a fool of herself again, in front of Jamie. She watched as he wrestled the bear to the ground.

'The school fair?' he said in a way that suggested he thought the chicken-pox had affected her memory. 'You said you'd take the kids, but then you were asleep, and we thought we should leave you to it.' He was obviously trying not to grin, and it seemed to be only with a great effort that he kept the look of concern on his face.

Freya blew out a breath. 'If I'd have seen the note I wouldn't have called the police, would I?' she said, stomping off in the direction of the lounge and throwing herself down on the sofa.

'Why did you call the police, Auntie Freya?' Benji said. 'Mummy says we should only do that if we're in trouble, but we weren't in trouble, we were at the fair. And I won the teddy bear. He's the biggest one I've seen!' His eyes were open wide, and Daisy beside him was nodding her head vigorously. Freya had hoped this would be a sign that the conversation was moving on, but no.

'Yes, Auntie Freya, why did you call the police?' Lily asked in the kind of innocent tone that had nothing to do with innocence.

'I panicked — I thought you'd been kidnapped or something.' Freya had mumbled the reply hoping no one would hear; but from the looks of the faces all staring at her, they had all heard every word.

There was silence for a moment, and then the laughter started. Freya shook her head as Lily threw herself onto the sofa next to her and laughed until she cried. Jamie had to sit down as he was literally bent over with deep booming gasps of laughter, and Benji and Daisy just looked a little bemused before they gave in to the infectious mood and giggled along too. Freya shrugged, feeling her grumpiness and embarrassment being pulled away from her by the sheer joy in the room, and joined in.

★ ★ ★

'I still can't quite believe you called the police,' Jamie said hours later, handing

210

Freya a glass of wine.

'I was a bit dozy from sleep,' she said, trying to sound hurt but failing miserably. 'You can just notch it up to another epic parenting fail on my account.'

He stared, and his face was serious for a moment. 'You think you're failing at this?'

'I'm pretty sure you were the first to point it out, Mr Barnes,' she said jokingly, but he looked embarrassed.

'Well, I was wrong. You're doing a great job.' He took a sip of his wine then, and Freya wondered if he had been about to say something else.

'Well, let's see . . . I failed to get either child to school on time for more than a week. My youngest niece got a bead stuck up her nose. We all got chickenpox, including me. And oh yes, the highlight of the experience — my eleven-year-old niece ran away in the middle of the night.'

'I think that's why they call parenting the hardest job in the world. You became an instant parent to three children, so don't beat yourself up.'

Freya blinked in surprise. Coming from Mr Barnes, even if he was being 'Jamie' right now, that was saying something. 'Thank you,' she said softly, and she suddenly realised how important it was to her that not only was she doing an okay job looking after the kids, but that he thought so too. She leaned back against him and he lifted an arm so that she could snuggle in. She wasn't sure why, but it felt like the most natural thing in the world to do.

'You're amazing, and I should've told you that before,' he said.

'I think that fact could be open to debate, but I'm curious — why didn't you?' She looked up now so that she could see his face and read his expression. With her head resting against his chest, she could feel him sigh, and she wondered if she had made another faux paux; if he would make an excuse and leave. She braced herself, but when he didn't move she allowed herself to relax. There was silence, so she allowed him that. Clearly he needed to think about his answer, and she was happy to let him, sure that he was going to finally share his story, which might explain some of his past behaviour.

'I fell in love with a parent once before,' he said softly, and Freya didn't have to see his face to know that he was lost in a time long gone. She squeezed his hand to show she was listening. 'I didn't just love her; I loved her kids. I was sure that we could be a family together. That's what I wanted, and I thought she wanted it too, so I let down my guard — and I fell hard. As it turns out, Melissa wasn't quite so convinced.'

Freya could feel Jamie's breaths coming faster, and she knew that the memory still brought him real pain.

'When she ended it, I promised myself I'd never let that happen to me again. The pain was unbearable. Not only had I lost the person I thought was the love of my life, but I'd lost my family too. I loved those kids like they were my own. And just like that — ' He clicked his fingers. ' — they were taken from me. I was just the ex-boyfriend. I didn't have any right to see them. Melissa's eldest, Bethany, was at my school, and so I still got to see her, but I've no idea what Melissa told her. She was by turns angry and bereft. Then six months later, Melissa met someone else and they moved away.'

Freya moved her arms so that she was encircling Jamie, giving him the best hug she could from where she lay. She tilted her head upwards so that he could see her face. 'I'm so sorry,' she said simply, knowing that no words could erase or even ease that kind of pain.

Jamie's face was stricken with the memory, but there was the smallest hint of a smile. 'Then I met you — so different, so sure of yourself, and so . . . well, let's just say slightly crazy.'

Freya tried to look hurt but couldn't manage it, and instead she giggled, her mind filled with all of her encounters with Mr Barnes.

'When I turned round and found you sitting on one of the infant's chairs, all dignified as if it were the most normal thing in the world . . . '

They both laughed now, and it was such a release of emotion for them both that they gave in to it.

'I was trying to be all grown up and responsible,' Freya managed to gasp between peals of laughter.

'It was then I knew that you were different; and despite my sensible head reminding me of what happened with Melissa, I think that was the moment I fell in love with you.' Jamie whispered the last part, and Freya was caught off guard.

'You love me?' she whispered back as she tried to pin down exactly how she felt about those words.

'I do,' Jamie said simply. He didn't have to ask the question, as it lay heavy in the air.

Freya considered those words carefully. How did she feel? She had to admit she had never felt so comfortable with someone, which was even more surprising after the start their relationship had had. She missed him when he wasn't there, and she got that funny feeling deep in her belly when he walked into a room.

'I love you too,' she said out loud, feeling the excitement of those words buzz through her brain and explode in her heart.

'Well that's a relief. It would've been super awkward if you said you couldn't stand the sight of me,' he whispered back, and they both chuckled. 'Stay with me, Freya Hardy. Forever?'

She smiled at the words before their meaning sunk in. She loved Jamie that much, she knew — but she had plans. Plans that she had already put on hold for the love of her family, but dreams that she was determined to chase nonetheless. The only problem was how to tell Jamie.

24

Freya chewed at her lip. The sound of Jamie's words had made her feel so blissfully happy, and then reality had struck home. She loved him, and he said that he loved her — but would he wait for her? She had worked so hard, and had so many places she wanted to go; and that hadn't changed, even if the rest of her life had.

'What are you thinking about?' Jamie asked, weaving his fingers between hers.

Freya swallowed. Was she really going to threaten her newfound happiness for a long-held dream? The thought made a tiny bubble of anger grow inside her. She shouldn't have to choose! If Jamie really loved her, then he would let her go. He would wait for her. Then another idea struck her. He could come with her! They could travel together. She could take him to all the places she had dreamed of and all the art she was dying to see, for real, hanging on a wall rather than as a glossy photograph.

'I'm thinking about travelling and all the places I want to go.' She made herself say the words out loud before she could change her mind. She knew that if she did, she would always resent Jamie, and that was no way to build a relationship.

'Maybe we could go together one day.'

He had uttered the fateful words, and Freya felt her heart contract from the pain those words meant. 'I'm going to leave when Astrid gets back.' She let the words hang in the air for a few moments. 'If you could come with me then?' Her heart pounded in her ears as she waited for him to reply.

'I can't,' he said softly. And in that moment Freya knew she had to put some distance between the two of them. She shuffled so that she was now sitting at one end of the sofa, her legs folded up underneath her, facing him.

She felt a slight sense of relief that he at least looked sad or wistful, one of the two.

His hand reached out and took hers. She wanted to snatch hers away but couldn't quite bring herself to do so; after all, perhaps he had a good reason for needing to stay. Perhaps one of his parents was sick and he needed to be close by.

'You have to understand Freya . . . my job.'

She turned her head away. She knew that Jamie loved his job and that it was important to him. It was one of the things that she had come to love about him. It took a real man to love other people's children; to care about how they grew and what they learned. But she knew she could not simply throw away all her dreams for a man who was not prepared to even give an inch. Relationships were about a partnership, giving and taking, and that was what she wanted — no, needed.

Freya found her feet and stood

before she had a chance to waver. She loved him, she knew it, but she wanted both love *and* her dreams. Maybe she was being unreasonable, but it was a fact she couldn't ignore. 'I understand,' she said, and poured herself some more wine. 'Coffee?'

'I don't think you do,' he said, reaching out for her hand as she walked past. This time she did shake it off.

'What's to understand?' she asked, trying desperately to keep the bitterness out of her voice. She felt like she had been promised so much only to have it taken away, like the tablecloth trick that magicians did. 'You have your dreams and I have mine. They aren't compatible, or at least they aren't right now. I'll be travelling for a year and then I'll be back.' She frowned. 'I'll be back here, and then maybe we can see if we both still want a relationship.' But she knew that it was unlikely. For all Jamie's words, it was clear what he wanted. He wanted someone who would stay right here; who had no dreams beyond being his girlfriend — and that was not her. Better to end it now before more time went by; before more hurt would be caused.

Although she had her back to him, she knew that he had stood up, and she knew deep in her gut that it was a bad sign. 'If that's what you want,' he said, and Freya knew that Mr Barnes was back. 'If you change your mind or want to discuss this, then let me know.' He walked past her without another word and let himself out the front door.

Freya stayed where she was, as if frozen in that moment. Inside her, a battle raged between the half that wanted to run after him and the half that told her she needed to follow her dreams or end up resenting him. The pain was too much, and she dropped to her knees. She raised a hand to her mouth to try and muffle the sobs, but she heard soft footsteps on the stairs and soon found herself pulled into the arms of her niece. Lily, just eleven years old, held her and smoothed her hair, without saying a word. She really was her mother's daughter.

★ ★ ★

Freya heard the children crashing around and hushing each other to be quiet. She rolled over in bed and smiled. She didn't blame them for being up so early — a squint at her phone told her it was five minutes past five — because today was the day.

She stared up at the ceiling. She couldn't believe that Astrid had been gone for nearly four months. They had seen her in that time, of course: Freya had taken the kids down to London, and Astrid had managed to come home for a weekend. But it wasn't the same as having her here permanently. Certainly not for the kids; and if Freya was honest, not for her either.

The time had passed quickly since that fateful evening with Jamie. There had been no more being late for school, and no other issues, so she'd had no reason to speak to Jamie and hadn't been summoned to his office. Part of her was a little sad about that. While she was sure that she'd made the right decision for both of them, it didn't mean that it hadn't come without pain, especially at night when she closed her eyes and all she could dream of was being in his arms.

But all that was about to change with Astrid's arrival home. Freya's tickets were all booked, her case was packed, and she was ready to head out to Paris, her first stop, in a week's time. That was what she needed to focus on, she told herself firmly as she slipped out of bed.

Downstairs was a sort of organised chaos that she had spent the last three months getting used to. The children obviously had a secret plan that involved making a welcome-home cake and painting a large banner. As a consequence, the kitchen was covered in a thin layer of flour, and every surface had something sticky on it. The table was covered in splotches of paint, but they had managed to write 'Welcome Home Mumy!' on it.

'There's two ems in 'mummy', dummy,' Lily was saying to Benji, one hand on her hip and her eyes rolling in exasperation.

'There *are* two ems,' Benji said in hurt confusion.

'Two ems in the middle,' Lily said, softening a little. 'I told you to let me deal with the spelling. I thought you were going to paint the dinosaurs.'

'I did!' Benji jabbed his paintbrush at a green blob which Freya could now see had the short arms of a T-rex.

'Looks perfect to me,' Freya said, walking into the kitchen with a smile. Lily and Benji froze as if they had been caught doing something very bad. 'Now why don't we let it dry and get cleared up. I think an extra-special treat for Mummy would be tidy bedrooms.'

Freya thought she would receive moans and groans, but instead the children scrambled upstairs, and by the loud banging of cupboard doors Freya could tell they were tidying up, or at least shoving everything on the floor into a cupboard. Not exactly tidy, but it would look good, as long as Astrid didn't open any doors.

25

No one could contain their excitement; even Lily was hopping from one foot to the other. Benji held one end of the banner and Lily the other, and Daisy was kneeling on the ground, peeking out from underneath it. The children had this part down pat, having welcomed their dad home from his deployments many times.

Freya glanced at the arrivals board one last time. 'Any minute now,' she said, and Daisy squealed while Benji stood on tiptoe, clearly determined to be the first to see the train wind its way around the bend.

The sound of screeching brakes hit their ears first, and then the train glided into the station. It was all Freya could do to prevent the children surging forward and getting lost in the scrum of people getting off the train. 'Hang on,' she said, reaching out a hand. 'Mummy will find us, remember.'

As Freya said the words, her sister seemed to materialise from the crowds. As if knowing what to expect, Astrid dropped to one knee and held out her arms. The children dropped the banner and ran forward, nearly knocking their mother backwards to the platform floor.

Freya felt the emotion build inside her and she knew she was going to cry. The children were full of sheer joy, the kind that only children can really express so openly; and the sight of Astrid with her children in her arms once more, laughing and crying at the same time, was too much. Freya shrugged and let herself have that happy cry. Minutes passed, and then it was Freya's turn to be hugged.

'Thank you,' Astrid whispered.

'No need,' Freya whispered back. 'That's what families do. You taught me that.'

* * *

It wasn't until the children were in bed that Astrid and Freya could finally talk, curled up on the sofa with a big bowl of rocky road ice cream to share.

'So, Lily tells me that your love life has not been uneventful,' Astrid said with that familiar sister-like twinkle in her eyes.

'I'd say it's been about as disastrous as it always is,' Freya said, trying to hold back the wave of misery that always accompanied thinking about Jamie.

Astrid read the change in mood and reached out an arm. Freya fell into a hug. 'Do you love him?' her sister asked softly.

'Yes,' Freya said between sobs. 'But I've dreamed of this trip for so long, and he wanted me to stay to give it up. I couldn't do that. I know I'd resent him for it, and then where would we be?'

'Did he say that? That he wanted you to stay?'

Freya frowned as she replayed the

conversation. 'No, but he said he wouldn't come with me.' She knew her voice sounded as sulky as Lily's when an adult pointed out something she didn't want to hear.

Astrid chuckled. 'Well that's not quite the same thing, is it?' she said gently.

'I'm not sure it makes much difference. I'm leaving in a week, and long-distance relationships never work.'

'Don't they?' Astrid said, raising an eyebrow and laughing.

Freya found herself joining in. 'Except for you and Mike,' she said between giggles. Astrid had that look in her eye, that thoughtful planning look. 'Please don't interfere,' Freya told her. 'I need to keep my mind focused on the trip, which is hard enough as it is. I don't need any fresh heartache or rejection.'

'Okay,' said her sister innocently, which Freya knew was not necessarily the agreement she was looking for.

'Please.'

Astrid held up both her hands as if admitting defeat. 'I won't talk to Mr Barnes about anything to do with you, I promise.'

Freya relaxed a little. She didn't think she could bear a repeat of the last conversation she'd had with Jamie. That one was seared into her mind and caused her pain every time she thought of it; and if she had to go through that again, she thought all she would be able to do was curl up in a ball and cry.

'I may need to speak to him about Benji, of course, but I promise I won't mention anything about you.'

Freya sat up and stared at her sister suspiciously, but Astrid looked as if she had taken on board Freya's words — although she knew that her sister had mastered the 'mum look' many years before she'd had her own children, when Freya was a teenager.

'Enough of that. I want to hear all your plans. I thought I could buy a poster map of the world, and the children and I could track you as you go,' Astrid said, ever the master at changing the subject.

* * *

Before she knew it, Freya found herself back at the train station, but this time it was to say goodbye. Lily and Benji unfurled a banner that said: 'Goodbye Anty Freya! We will miss you!' Obviously Benji had been in charge of spelling again, and it made her smile despite the butterflies of anxiety in her stomach. She was going, she really was. No more dreaming and making plans — she was really going on an adventure.

'Send us lots of postcards,' said Benji, jumping up and down, 'so we can put pins in our map and see where you are.'

Freya knelt down and pulled her nephew into a hug. 'Of course I will. And look after your mum and the girls until your daddy gets home,' she whispered more softly. Then she pulled herself from Benji's tight embrace and smiled at him. He looked solemn for a moment but then returned her smile. Freya knew why. Only the thought of Daddy coming home could bring that kind of light to his eyes. 'Only thirty-four days,' she said.

Benji rolled his eyes. 'It's thirty-three, Auntie Freya. You don't count today,' he said with exaggerated patience.

Freya winked at him to show that she was joking, and he laughed. She reached for Lily next, who surprisingly didn't resist the public display of affection that Freya had assumed would not be 'cool' for an eleven-year-old.

'I'll miss you,' Lily whispered.

'I'll miss you too, but I'll be back.'

Lily drew back and now looked a little awkward. 'Thanks for everything,' she mumbled before turning her attention to Benji, who was struggling to hold the banner by himself. Freya smiled. Lily had been hard work but completely worth it, and Freya felt like she had connected with her niece properly for the first time in a while.

She didn't have time to ponder this any further as she was pulled into a fierce, tight hug from Astrid, who also had Daisy in her arms. 'Oww, Mummy, you're squishing me!' the little girl protested.

'Sorry, Daisy,' Astrid said, pulling back a little. 'Give Auntie Freya a kiss.'

Daisy leaned in and gave Freya her last chocolatey kiss for what would be a while.

'Bye, Daisy. Bye, Astrid,' Freya said as the train drew in behind her.

'Text me when you get to Paris,' Astrid said, her face a little pinched with the anxiety she was obviously feeling.

'I will, I promise,' Freya said as she heaved her backpack through the train doors. She quickly dumped her rucksack in the baggage store and then found a seat by the window. The beeping told her the doors were closing and the train was about to leave. She searched and quickly found her little family group, arms around each other and waving frantically. She giggled and waved back and kept waving until they were out of sight, thinking of all the stories she would have to tell them when she got back home.

26

Freya still couldn't believe she was on her adventures. It had been a dream for so long that she kept expecting herself to wake up. She had been away for nearly six weeks and had travelled across France, visiting all the places and art galleries she had ever dreamed of; and now she was in Florence, Italy. She was staying in a small hotel in the oldest part of the city, overlooking a narrow cobbled street from her tiny balcony.

The workers of the city were up making coffee and preparing for their day. Freya was headed to the Uffizi gallery, one of her top places to visit to see famous Italian paintings in the flesh, and she couldn't wait. She planned to stay the whole day there and possibly the next, to give her time to take it all in.

She slipped past the tiny reception desk to avoid a long and protracted conversation with the lovely but talkative owner and made her way out into the street. By now it was bustling, but she didn't mind. She loved to walk slowly and soak it all in. She smiled as she walked, thinking that sometimes reality could be so much better than dreams.

As she approached the heart of Florence, where the gallery was, she delved into her bag for her guidebook and flicked to the introduction. Even though she must have read it a thousand times already, she wanted to read about the building as she walked through the high stone arches. She looked up, shading her eyes against the sun so that she could see the intricate architecture, but she was being jostled by a large crowd of tourists who all had their hearts and their feet set on reaching the entrance before anyone else.

She sighed just a little, made her way

to the low stone steps, and found herself a corner to tuck herself into before turning back to her guidebook. A shadow passed in front of her and she felt someone sit down beside her. She shuffled a little, feeling that stranger was a little too close; but then this was Italy, she mused.

'*Ciao!*' a voice sounded beside her. Freya was getting used to the friendliness of the nation she found herself in, but she couldn't help but sigh a little. She really wanted to focus on the art rather than making friends with strange men. She looked up briefly and gave a smile, hoping that her message would be felt loud and clear.

'*Mi sei mancata.*'

Freya stopped reading again. Either her ears were deceiving her, or that was not a very Italian accent; not that she knew what the words meant. She looked up again, and the guidebook fell from her hands. The thud as it hit the stone floor made her jump a little.

'I said I missed you.'

Freya blinked once and then twice. Jamie was sitting next to her on the steps of the Uffizi Gallery, and now she knew she had to be dreaming. It couldn't be true. Jamie was in England, following his dreams to teach and find someone to settle down with.

'I know my accent needs work, but could you say something, please?' His voice had a tinge of worry now, and Freya jumped at his touch as he reached out for her hand with his.

'You can't be here,' she whispered softly.

'I can go if you want.' There it was, the tinge of Mr Barnes, and Freya turned to look at him properly for the first time.

'You're really here?' she asked, thinking that any minute she was going to wake up and feel the familiar ache of the distance between them.

He smiled now, and it seemed he had finally picked up that Freya was confused and uncertain. 'Yes,' he said, squeezing her hand once more, 'I'm really here.'

'How?' was the first question that fought its way to the front of her bemused mind.

'Well, I got a train. Astrid dropped me off,' he added with a grin. 'And then I got on a plane. You send a text to Astrid every day, so I knew where you were going to be, and I thought I'd surprise you.'

Freya swallowed and tried to make sense of what she had just been told. Jamie was here, here with her in Florence. How was that even possible? 'But school?' she asked.

'It's the summer holidays.'

Freya nodded. 'So you came all this way to visit me?' She wanted to know everything. Her heart skipped at the thought that he was here, but she needed to know more; needed to know what his plans were.

'I have five weeks, so I plan to travel with you, if you'll let me?'

'But you didn't want to come.'

Freya's voice came out sounding like a child's, but she couldn't keep all the hurt of their parting from it.

'That's not exactly what I said.'

She glanced up at him again, wondering if she had upset him or if Mr Barnes was back, but his face was soft and he smiled at her.

'You didn't really give me much chance to explain what I was thinking, and you seemed so certain that you wanted me to walk away. So I did.'

'That was the last thing I wanted. But I couldn't stay with you and not do this.' She waved her hands. 'I would've resented you, and I couldn't bear that. It would've been worse than the pain of losing you.' She said the last words to the stone floor, unable to look Jamie in the eye, fearing she would give away just how much pain she had been in.

She felt a hand gently lift her chin, and in Jamie's face she could see a mirror of her own feelings. 'I love you, Freya Hardy,' he said firmly. 'And because I love you, I never want you to

240

give up on your dreams. Not for anyone, and not for me.'

He leaned in and kissed her: at first a brush of his lips against hers, and then more deeply, speaking of the time and distance that had kept them apart. 'I would've told you that had you given me the chance,' he said.

Freya looked rueful. He was right, of course; but then, why hadn't he tried to speak to her again?

It was as if he could read her mind. 'Your sister set me straight. Marched right into the office on her first day back and demanded to speak to me.'

Freya giggled, since Jamie looked quite shocked and nonplussed at the memory.

'She told me right out that I was an idiot.'

Freya laughed again and found herself drawn into Jamie's arms. She snuggled her head under his chin, and it felt like she was where she was supposed to be.

'She said *you* were an idiot, too.'

Now they both laughed. As always, Astrid had a point.

'She said that if it was clear to her eleven-year-old that we were in love, it was madness that we two grown-ups couldn't figure it out.'

'I don't think that bit was the problem,' Freya said to his chest as she listened to his heartbeat and the words he spoke rumble in her chest.

'No, she also said we were both too stubborn to admit we were wrong, and that we'd singularly failed to give each other time to explain exactly what we meant.'

Freya laughed. 'That sounds like Astrid.'

Jamie kissed her on the top of her head and she ran an arm around his back, so that she was holding him too. 'She told me to get a grip,' he said, 'and that if I really loved you, I'd figure out a way to make it work.'

'And so you came here,' Freya said, asking a question as well as making a statement.

'So I came here. I booked my flight that evening for the first day of the summer holidays. Astrid told me where you planned to be and then texted me this morning with your exact location.'

'I love you,' Freya said simply. They were the words she had been longing to say to him since their angry parting. 'Going away on this trip doesn't mean I love you any less.'

'I know that. I've always known that, but your sister was right. I was too stubborn and hurt to come back and speak to you after that day. I've been hurt before, and I thought I was protecting myself.'

'I never meant to hurt you,' Freya whispered.

'I never meant to hurt you either,' Jamie said to her. 'When I thought about it, I wasn't hurt that you wanted to leave. I was hurt that you didn't seem to want me with you.'

'I told you I wanted you to come,' Freya said, drawing away slightly.

Jamie leaned in and kissed her

indignant nose. 'I know you did, but the reality was I couldn't. As a teacher, I have to give a half-term's worth of notice. I'm locked into my current contract until Christmas.'

Freya bit her lip and felt colour rise in her cheeks that had nothing to do with the hot sun. 'Oh.'

'If we weren't both a pair of stubborn idiots, I would've explained that to you. Made you listen.'

Freya winced at the thought of the pain she had caused him. 'I'm sorry,' she said.

'I think we've both established that we're sorry, my love.' He pulled her back into his arms.

'Let's make a pact here on the steps of this gallery to make time to listen to each other. And to stop being idiots.'

Jamie chuckled. 'We can do that too.' And he kissed her again.

27

The five weeks flew by. Freya repeatedly vowed to herself to enjoy all the moments and not waste their precious time together worrying about the day that Jamie would leave her and go back home. It seemed so strange now to even think about travelling without him, even though that was what she had planned and what she had been doing until Jamie's unexpected arrival at the steps of the Uffizi Gallery. She tried telling herself firmly that she would be fine, but the truth was that the idea of the trip had lost some of its shine at the thought of being apart for another nine months.

They had travelled across Spain, back into France, and were now in Holland, heading for the Kröller-Müller Museum in Otterlo. One final day together, and then Jamie was catching a flight back to the UK. They were strolling hand in hand around the outdoor sculpture park, and it was breathtaking, but somehow not enough to take Freya's mind off the next day.

'This one looks like a dancing cow,' Jamie said, gesturing to what could only be called an abstract piece of art.

Freya elbowed him in the ribs, knowing that he was trying to make her laugh and welcoming the distraction. 'Slightly concerning, since it's supposed to represent the face of love,' she retorted.

Jamie made a great show of consulting the guidebook. 'Oh, still looks like a dancing cow to me. Maybe that's what the sculptor thinks love looks like.'

Freya rolled her eyes. Jamie had shown a keen interest to learn about the art that she loved, but he was a traditionalist at heart. He liked art to look like what it was supposed to be portraying.

'I think *this* is what love looks like,'

he said with dramatic flair, bowing low before her.

Freya knew she was blushing. Other people, serious people interested in art, had turned to stare at them, some muttering in disapproval. 'Give over,' she said with mock crossness.

Jamie grinned and then gestured her to a bench, which was placed so that those with tired feet had a spectacular view of the sculptures. 'I have something to tell you,' he said.

'Oh yes?' Freya said with one eyebrow raised. No doubt it was some other amusing comment about modernist art.

'Actually, it's a surprise.'

Now Freya frowned, trying to work out what was going on. 'Oh?' she said, and tried to infuse her words with the sense that she was curious but not overly bothered. For a moment she thought he was going to try and make her guess; but whatever it was, he seemed all of a sudden impatient for her to know.

'Well, I've been thinking, and nine months seems like a long time to be apart.'

Freya's heart missed a beat as she wondered once more if he would ask her to come home before her trip was over. For a moment she pondered how she felt about that.

'It's not what you think,' he said, holding up his hands. 'I'm not asking you to come back with me.' He looked worried and so she smiled, though she still had no idea where this was going.

'So I thought I'd join you at Christmas, if you'd like.' He made the last comment rather shyly, and Freya couldn't resist throwing her arms around his neck. As if she wouldn't want to spend Christmas with him!

'Are you sure?' she said. 'I mean there's your family . . . '

'Freya, I've spent the last thirty-three years with my family. I'm sure they can cope with one Christmas without me.'

She squealed at the thought and kissed him. He kissed her back but broke away first, laughing at her puzzled expression. 'I haven't finished,' he said.

'What could be better than you spending Christmas with me on my travels?'

'Well, I was thinking that coming out at Christmas and staying with you till the end of your trip might be nice.' He said it casually, as if he was suggesting a restaurant they should have dinner at.

Freya just gawped at him. She knew her mouth was hanging open and she must look like a rabbit in headlights, but she couldn't help it. She was sure she had heard him wrong.

'Only if you're okay with that, obviously. I know it's been your dream, and you didn't necessarily factor me into that.'

She kissed him then, full on the lips, partly because she couldn't resist the urge and partly because she wanted him to stop talking. 'There's nothing I'd love more,' she said seriously. She needed him to know that was one hundred percent the truth. 'But what about school?'

He shrugged. 'I gave them the required term's notice.'

Freya leaned in and kissed him again, running her hands through his hair. 'But you've given up your job for me?'

Now it was his turn to look serious. 'Freya Hardy, I love you. When will you get that into your stubborn head?' He locked eyes with her, and she knew that he too was speaking from his heart. 'And besides, they want me back, so they've let me take a career break.' His eyes sparkled with mischief, and Freya had to fight the urge to punch him on the arm. 'That is, if you're happy to make a home with me there, once this particular adventure is over.'

Freya tilted her head to one side. 'There's nothing I want more,' she whispered; and before she knew it, he had found his feet and she felt herself twirled around in the air.

This time she threw her head back

and laughed, ignoring the stares of the other visitors, lost in her very own dream come true.

WISHES CAN COME TRUE

Angela Britnell

Meg Harper is shocked when the man she knows as Lucca Raffaele, who stood her up in Italy the previous summer, arrives to stay at her family home in Tennessee — this time calling himself her step-cousin, Jago Merryn . . . Jago is there to acquire a local barbecue business, but discovering the woman who came close to winning his heart is only one of the surprises in store for him. Can they move past their mistrust and seize a second chance for their wishes to come true?

CHRISTMAS TREES AND MISTLETOE

Fay Cunningham

The idea of another family Christmas fills Fran with dread, particularly when she is asked to pick up her mother's latest charity case and bring him along. But Ryan Conway is not what she was expecting. He is looking after his young niece while his sister is in hospital, and Fran decides the pair of them may not be such bad company after all. Then, once the festivities are in full swing, Santa arrives unexpectedly — and Fran's life changes forever . . .

LOVE UNEXPECTED

Sarah Purdue

After being jilted by her fiancé, Nurse Jenny Hale decides to escape the well-meaning but suffocating sympathy of her friends and family by taking her honeymoon alone. On her journey to the Caribbean island of St. Emilie, a crisis throws her together with Doctor Luc Buchannan — who she finds herself falling for. But Luc also carries a heavy burden from his past. Is it possible for the doctor and the nurse to heal each other's hearts?

IT'S NEVER TOO LATE

Wendy Kremer

When Rebecca Summer is contracted to work as a temporary secretary for businessman Luca Barsetti on the Italian island of San Andrea, she thinks she can handle it — even though she was infatuated with him eight years ago at university. Much to her dismay, however, she finds that Luca's charms have not dimmed with time, and he appears to return her feelings. But she's now a confident, independent woman, far too sensible to fall head over heels for him again . . . isn't she?

WISH UPON A STAR

Charlotte McFall

Abandoning her life and starting anew seemed like the best option for Claire. Now, seven years on, she is helping to run a successful nightclub in Newcastle, and her daughter Gemma, boss Lee and his wife Cari are all the family she needs. The last person she expects to see is her ex — who just happens to be rock star Mark Crofts. No one has ever taken Claire's place in his heart. But can he win her back?

IMPETUOUS NURSE

Alison Bray

Nurse Lynn Avery has a reputation for being a practical joker, which she uses to conceal her unhappiness after her recent break-up. But she cannot remain in the wilderness; and although Doctor Vince Braddock professes his love for her, it is Doctor Paul Morgan who has her under his spell. When Lynn accepts that she is in love, her problems are only starting, as shadows creep back into her life. Then Paul begins to show an interest in Della Tate, and matters go from bad to worse . . .